BURIED IN GRI

By C.G. Buswell

Also, by C.G. Buswell

Novels

The Grey Lady Ghost of the Cambridge Military Hospital: Grey and
Scarlet 1

The Drummer Boy: Grey and Scarlet 2

Short Stories

Christmas at Erskine

Halloween Treat

Angelic Gift

Burnt Vengeance

The Release

Christmas Presence

For my wonderful daughter Abigail, beautiful and strong in so many ways. I love you.

Chapter 1

Hamish stirred in his sleep, wrapping the duvet around his body like a cloak and taking the warmth of it with him, much to his wife's chagrin. Alison too stirred because of the chilled draft this movement caused and then she heard the faint double knocking from afar. '*Probably that stupid old man around the corner again, banging his shed doors or wheelie bins lids, why he couldn't just close them quietly, like a normal person, especially at this unearthly hour, she didn't know. It was almost as if he liked waking up the neighbourhood.*' She sighed as she looked across at the subdued light of her digital clock that shone out the time, one in the morning. '*Who in their right mind goes out to their shed and bangs around at this time of the night?*' she angrily further thought.

Gentle snoring came from her husband as he wrapped himself further into the white dove-decorated duvet, almost as if he was attempting to cocoon himself within the feathery down against the harshness of the Aberdeenshire winter weather. It made Alison think of a hibernating bear, especially as she knew the snoring would get louder. She gave a gentle chuckle to herself, though inside she was fuming that her nasty neighbour had awakened her again. *'If only I could be like Hamish,'* she thought, *'he could fall asleep on a washing line and sleep through a nuclear attack.'*

There was a further knock, this time a louder, treble knocking, followed by a thudding four beats, much louder and more insistent. Someone wanted her attention. 'Hamish!' she urgently cried out into the darkness of the room.

He turned to face her, rolling over automatically in his sleep, his subconscious not yet acknowledging her urgency.

The knocking continued, another persistent four beats, almost as if someone was beating out a tune on a… 'DOOR, THERE'S SOMEONE AT THE DOOR HAMISH!' she now shouted, to awaken her husband.

He sat bolt upright, instantly awake and ready to face the night attack to their safety. His long forgotten military training instinctively kicking in. It felt to his muddled mind that he was in a slit trench, back in the plains of Salisbury, and the dawn warning of "STAND TO!" had been shouted by the sentries. But as his head cleared, he knew that this was no army stand-to-arms order. 'What? What's wrong love?'

'Can't you hear it, you daft lump? Someone's at the door!'

'Och, it's probably just Paul, forgotten his keys, the stupid sod!'

The banging continued as Hamish reluctantly dragged himself out of his comfortable and warm bed and slipped on his heavy tartan dressing gown. He fastened the tasselled belt firmly around his waist, as if to dissipate his anger at the foolishness of his son's forgetfulness. He walked over to the window and looked down into the driveway to see if Paul's car was there. The rain was pelting down onto the lock block paving of his half-empty driveway, giving it a silky sheen in the subdued moonlight. His eye was drawn across the road where a lone police car sat. The street lamp shone down its eerie dim yellow light casting a shadow across the vehicle, lengthening its unwanted and intrusive presence. It was empty of driver and passenger. His mouth instantly dried and he felt the long-forgotten tightening in his stomach and groin as terror

8

swept through him like a passing fighter jet on a low
sortie. 'No, no no!' he exclaimed involuntary. 'Please. God
no!'

Alison jumped out of bed, instinctively knowing that
something was awry, not having seen her husband with
such a horrified reaction before. She grabbed her dressing
gown from the hook behind the bedroom door, reached for
the handle and flung open the door. The banging grew
louder and more insistent as she ran down the stairs,
closely followed by her shaking husband. He knew that
they were about to receive the news that they themselves
had given to so many families over the years. Helplessness
flooded through him, first as a sudden icy coldness and
then as a creeping chilliness that stayed like an unwelcome
guest. He followed his wife down the stairs and could see
the luminous yellow jackets with blue patches through the
frosted glass of their front door as Alison fumbled with the

9

house keys. The bulky shapes outside turned around, as if to keep warm from the Scottish winter's night. This movement allowed Hamish to see the rectangular blue stripe across their backs. Though the frosted glass did not afford him the decency of being able to read the words, he knew what they read and knew the purpose of their visit. This was the knock on the door that every parent dreaded, and he was certain that no warmth would ever enter their lives again.

Hamish switched on the lights that Alison had rushed past as he took, what felt to him, the long walk to the door. The two figures outside turned around and faced the door, preparing themselves for one of their duties that no-one liked. The Knock, as it was known in every station throughout the UK. Every officer dreaded this order and reluctantly had to accept this duty. It had to be done sometime in their career. '*Please God, let them be at the wrong house,*' prayed Hamish silently. He reached across to Alison's shaking hands that jangled the keys like an elaborate baby's rattle. He inhaled heavily as if to prepare himself for what was to come, and to control his shaking hands. '*Be strong for her,*' he commanded himself. 'Here, love, let me,' he gently said as he took both her hands in his and soothingly stroked them with his thumbs. 'Give me the keys,' he reinforced to her.

Alison nodded, dread had overcome her ability to speak, though her lips were quivering as if in silent prayer too. She drew comfort from the muscular hands of her husband, not wanting to release herself from their protective grip. Reluctantly she dropped the keys and felt the removal of her husband's warmth as he took them from her and reached out and inserted the key and turned the lock mechanism. She couldn't help but consider this action to be a turning point in their lives from which they may never recover.

As Hamish opened the door a draft of wind danced around their sockless feet and up their pyjamas. Both police officers immediately removed their hats and displayed solemn expressions. 'Mr and Mrs Dewart?' asked the older one, a touch of greyness streaked through his hair added to his authority.

'Y, yes officer,' replied Hamish hesitantly, before finding his voice with a forceful cough and throat clearing, 'why are you here?'

'Can we come in please Mr Dewart?' replied the older of the duo, his right arm outstretched and pointing into the lobby, reinforcing his polite request.

'Aye, of course officer, but why are you here? Please tell us?'

The police officers quietly made their way into the family home and out of the harsh night's weather whilst with forced dignity ignored Hamish's questions. They closed the front door with an almost inaudible click. Their arms remained stretched out as they silently ushered the couple through their own home. They took several steps into the hallway and lowered their heads when they reached the chandelier type light shade.

'Is my son okay, is it about Paul?' begged Alison, dropping her dressing gown to the floor, as her hands went to her ears, as if to shelter herself from the bad news to come.

The younger officer, about Paul's age, had noted Alison's dread and reached down for the dressing gown, and draped it over his arms whilst his colleague pointed behind her, to their lounge. 'Please, can we go through there, I'd like you to sit down.'

Paternal terror swept through Hamish as he recalled his army nursing days and the number of times he had asked wives, husbands, mothers and fathers to do the same, for the shock hits like a sledgehammer to the spine and radiates emotional pain throughout the body. This police officer did not want Alison to faint at the news he knew he had brought to the family home.

The police officer expertly guided them through to the lounge and sat Alison down and pointed to the other armchair, 'Mr Dewart, please sit down as well, I'm afraid it is bad news.'

Alison's hands went to her mouth as a maternal scream released itself as if from deep within her womb. She continued to wail as Hamish, who had ignored the officer's orders, walked over to her, knelt, stretched over to his childhood sweetheart, and held her close. He allowed her to howl as he stroked her hair, her back and then just held her, as if to protect her from the reality of this visit. He said nothing because he could find no words of comfort. Instead he whispered a gentle shh sound, just like he did when Paul was a toddler and woke through the night after a bad dream. Hamish knew that this was just the start of their nightmare from which they may never awaken.

The older police officer patiently watched as husband and wife took and received comfort from each other. He nodded to his younger colleague, two weeks into his probation period after the police college, to confirm to him that he was doing well. He then pointed to the empty sofa and both officers quietly settled down on it, despite their stab vests riding up above their shoulders as they hit their hips. Both discretely turned off their radios as they saw Paul's face smiling down to them from the family portrait above the mantelpiece.

'I, I'm al, all right now Hamish,' she shivered as her husband withdrew his comforting embrace. She stood up, ready to confront the bad news head on. 'Please tell us why you are here officers? Is our son okay? He's on nightshift and sometimes comes home early.'

'I'm so sorry Mr and Mrs Dewart, I'm afraid Paul was involved in a car accident and, there is no easy way to say this, I'm so sorry, but Paul died at the scene.'

The pallor faded from the couple, their faces went ashen white as their world collapsed around them, here in their family home, where they had brought up their son and daughter. In this room, Paul and his sister, Bella, had laughed in joy when they opened their Christmas presents, had sung Happy Birthday to each other, and even the family dog, Captain, over the last two decades. Paul had kissed his mother goodnight here so many times and now he would never set foot in their home again. The parents reached out to each other and grasped their white cold hands and then embraced the cuddle of grief that so many families had to enact and would, sadly, continue to perform. Their energy drained along with their pallor and Hamish gently sat his wife back down onto her armchair. He found the strength to ask the younger officer, 'could you please wrap the dressing gown around my wife, I shall just pop out and switch the heating on. It's ever so cold.'

The probationer leapt up, eager to help. He was keen to do something physical to help, whilst Hamish walked through to the kitchen, his legs like jelly, almost as if he had run a marathon and was taking the last difficult few steps. He made it through to the kitchen and had to lean on the wall for a few minutes, taking deep breaths whilst his soul cried out to his God. He could hear the younger police officer helping his crying wife. He was making soothing noises whilst giving gentle commands to help her into the warmth of her garment. Hamish then found the strength to reach out and turn the thermostat to twenty-one degrees as his body failed him and his shoulders shook and his whole essence shuddered. He cried and screamed inwardly as tears flowed down his cheeks, forming deep rivulets of emotional pain that burned deep to his inner being. His son, his flesh, his blood, his first-born, and his beloved creation was gone, and with him, his whole world had shattered and could never be repaired, ever. Several minutes passed before he could compose himself, as he willed himself to stop and to put on a brave face for his dear wife. He walked over to the ornately carved Welsh dresser and took off a piece of kitchen roll from the wooden roller, made by Paul at school woodwork class, and wiped his tears and then blew his nose. He slowly breathed in and out to compose himself once more and returned to the lounge.

'What happened to Paul?' he asked the officers, as he walked into the room. He noticed that the two police officers were looking down at the blue carpet, almost as if they were trying to match up the white square patterns in the weave, to take away their awkwardness that they were feeling at the weeping woman before them. Paul made his way to be with his wife, to be her rock once more.

The older one nodded again to his colleague who stated, 'At approximately 0030 hours your son Paul was driving on the A90 when he crashed his car and was killed instantly.' There was another nod from the older officer, as if prompting him of the words he'd rehearsed earlier. 'He wouldn't have suffered. It was quick, he wouldn't have felt anything.'

Hamish walked over to his wife, sat on the arm of her chair, leaned down and took her into his shoulder and enveloped her with as much comfort as he could hopelessly convey. He sighed, his heart weighing heavily with the inevitability of it all, and spoke over her shoulders, 'I've delivered that line many a time in my duties as a nurse. Quite often it was far from being honest, there was sometimes a great deal of pain and suffering. Please just tell me the truth. We are both old army nurses, so nothing you say can upset us any further than we already are.'

The policemen looked at each other and the older officer took the lead. 'I'm so sorry for your loss Mr Dewart, that's all we know now. There are other officers at the scene now, performing their crash investigations.'

'Was there anyone else involved?' demanded Hamish.

'I'm afraid we can't let you know until the investigation team have finished. We know so very little now.'

'I see,' replied Hamish, his thoughts jumbling and tossing in his troubled head. He took a deliberate deep breath in and exhaled slowly before continuing, 'Paul was a careful driver, especially at night when he often took work mates home, was he alone in the car?'

'We think so, it seems that he was returning to his work, after dropping off one of the young girls who missed her last bus home.'

'So why did he crash, it's not icy out there.'

'I wish I could tell you more, but I can't, but we do have some questions we need to ask you, just to verify that it is Paul. I'm so sorry to be so intrusive at this sad time.' The older officer cast his eyes quickly to his colleague, who took the hint and withdrew his notebook from his pocket.

Hamish ignored the request and instead asked, 'can we please see our son first, I need to know that it's him and that you haven't made a mistake.' Alison nodded in silent agreement, tears streamed down her face as she clung to a tissue that the kind young officer had given her when

Hamish went alone into the kitchen. It was soaked through. She needed to see her son and hold him whilst his spirit was still nearby, she knew this to be silly nursing superstition, but all the same she agreed with her husband.

'I'm so sorry, Mr and Mrs Dewart, there hasn't been a mistake. We are one-hundred-per-cent sure that it is Paul. He will be taken to the Queen Street Mortuary in Aberdeen, as soon as the crash investigators have done what they need to do. Please be assured that his dignity will be maintained at all times and that he'll be handled as gently as possible.'

Hamish nodded knowingly, he'd attended enough of those investigations whilst overseas. His thoughts went back to Belize, when he was stationed at the Hospital in Airport Camp and he was part of the Field Surgical Team. He'd attended the scene of a road accident when a four-tonne truck, carrying a unit of Gurkhas, had overturned down into an embankment. All had died at the scene when the petrol tank and spare jerrycans of fuel had blown-up and caused an inferno. They had not died quickly. He, and the other rescuers, had had to stand back and watch because of the live rounds of ammunition and grenades that had exploded every few seconds around the burning truck. He recoiled at the long-dormant memories, his nostrils flared as a never forgotten memory made him smell their charred flesh, skin that had burned deep and long and which he had had to touch and carry. Charred and blackened limbs had snapped off the corpses, as easily as twigs from a tree branch. This sound reverberated around his head like a teasing devil watching from the outskirts of his mind. He shook at the memory he had worked so hard at compartmentalising, despite long sessions with a psychologist. He realised that the unpleasant side of things would have to be done for his dear son, measurements, photographs and more. 'Okay,' he reluctantly replied, shoulders visibly sagging in resigned acceptance as reality set in, 'please ask your questions.'

The nod again and the younger police officer held up his black book and pen.

'When did you last see Paul?'

Alison started sobbing again and Hamish drew her closer so that he could bring his other arm around to cuddle and comfort her. 'This evening, he had his tea and then got ready for work.'

The officer wrote the details down, once again grateful for something physical to do.

'Are you sure it's him? He drove so carefully,' insisted Hamish.

'I'm so sorry Mr Dewart, it really is Paul, I knew him from his work. We'd pop in for food sometimes during our breaks and I've had to take statements from him about abusive drunks and shoplifters.'

Hamish grimaced. 'He loved that job, he worked his way up to night manager. We were very proud of him,' he managed to say before breaking into tears of his own. His wife held onto him even more strongly, now returning the comfort, a heart-wrenching example of their equal marriage.

'Yes, he did well, especially at such a young age. He was...' prompted the police officer apparently expertly, a tip he'd learnt at Tulliallan Castle, during his College role-playing sessions.

'22,' replied Alison, taking over parental duties whilst Hamish composed himself once more.

The officer wrote the information down. 'Could you please confirm his date of birth,' he hesitated, uncomfortable at seeing the father crying deep sobs of grief, 'er, Mrs Dewart.'

'The 21st of July 1996,' said Hamish, now composing himself. He withdrew from the embrace and took his wife's hands, not at all surprised to find they were icy cold. 'The happiest day of our lives, along with the birth of Bella a year later.' He looked into his wife's eyes and tried to express the love he had always felt for her, though he knew her life would never have joy again. He vowed to now stay strong for her. As if to confirm this thought she said to him, 'Oh God, how can we tell Bella? This is going to break her heart, they were the best of friends, not just brother and sister.' The couple looked at each other, leaving the question in the air unanswered.

Hamish broke off their gaze and looked back to the police officer and anticipated his next question by saying, 'He was born in the Akrotiri Military Hospital, in the Royal Air

Force Base in Cyprus. I was serving in the tri-service wards at The Princess Mary's Hospital. Two army midwives delivered him. He was 6 pounds 8 ounces, a weight I've never forgotten. A fine set of lungs on him,' his bottom lip started to quiver, unnoticed by the police officer who was busy writing the details down, grateful that the information had been readily given and that he'd not had to ask too many intrusive questions.

'Are you sure that it's Paul, he is too young to die,' pleaded Alison, 'he drove a red Volkswagen Golf, he saved up for ages for it. On his days off he'd wash and shine it, even the tyres got a good polish with some special stuff he bought at Halfords. He was so proud of it.' She turned to her husband and briefly smiled without joy in her eyes, 'if only he'd kept his bedroom as tidy!'

The officer, scribbled the colour, make and model down. 'I'm afraid so Mrs Dewart, I so wish it wasn't, but yes, that's the make, model and colour of the car. The licence number is registered to this address. I'm so sorry,' he repeated and looked like he truly meant it, he'd obviously been like other people and was caught up in the infectious happiness that Paul had radiated. Their son had touched so many lives and brought nothing but joy. He hoped the job would get easier after tonight, the Tulliallan College had prepared him for this awful responsibility. But telling parents that they'd never see their son alive again was just terrible, but not as awful as their lives would now be for years to come.

Noticing his colleague's reverie, the supervising police officer interjected 'Can I make you both a cup of tea?'

'No. I'll do that when you have gone, unless either of you would like one?' replied Hamish.

'No, we are good, thank you. That's all our questions for now. I'm so sorry again,' he looked back to the family portrait proudly taking centre stage in the lounge. 'Paul was a handsome chap, and I'm sure he was a credit to you both. It's usual for a police-liaison officer to contact you, probably after 8am, and by telephone. He or she will be your point of contact if you need any help or advice. He or she will also take you to the Chapel of Rest, where you can see Paul and then will ask you to formally identify that it is him. I'm afraid it will be behind a glass wall, please prepare yourselves that you won't be able to hold your son. I'm so sorry to leave you like this. Please do also make use of our 101-telephone service if you have any questions at any time Mr and Mrs Dewart.'

'Thank you, officer, yes,' replied Hamish, a determined expression in his eyes, 'I just have one question before you go, where exactly was the crash?'

Chapter 2

Two pairs of thick boots marched briskly up the driveway as the officers leant into the wind that drove the harsh rain into their faces, nipping at their exposed skin like frantic crabs trying to escape a fisherman's net. The younger officer cast a quick look behind him, towards the grief-stricken couple's semi-detached house. He was distracted by movement and light from the neighbour's window and was in time to see an aged hand hastily turn back the curtain, leaving the tell-tale signs of fluttering fabric in its wake.

The older policeman did not falter in his step, nor look behind, but said with authority and knowledge, 'the curtain-twitcher next door?'

'Yes, but how did you know?'

'There is always one, and none across the road are looking out. They are sensible enough to be fast asleep at this unearthly hour.'

They reached their car and quietly got in and sat down. In unison they turned back on their personal radio units and sighed. 'Does it get any easier?' asked the younger police officer?'

'I wish I could say that it does, but it doesn't. I've been to dozens of homes like this. The reactions are all different, but usually you get lots of crying and screaming, which is a normal reaction to an abnormal situation. After all, we've just gone in and destroyed that family's lives with the news we've had to deliver. Sometimes you just get a shocked response, and you must confirm the death repeatedly as a parent grasps at the slim chance that a mistake has been made. There's never a mistake in my experience. Poor folks. Either way, they have a long road of grief ahead of them, I don't envy them that lonely journey.'

His colleague sighed and switched on the car's ignition. The vehicle gently purred into life as an array of instruments glowed green before him, like a clowder of cats looking back at them. 'McDonalds?'

'We've certainly earned it, let's get out of here and get some coffee, my treat. You did well back there, you've a lovely sensitive nature about you. Don't let the job make you cynical and hardened like some others, you need the soft touch sometimes. The way you handled the questions was so delicate, well done.'

The probationer beamed as bright as the car's headlamps as he happily drove off, on their way to the drive-through of their favourite night-time snack outlet. He couldn't wait for tonight's donut. He hoped that they had the chocolate filled ones in stock, he licked his lips in anticipation.

Hamish stroked his wife's hair, taking his time to go slowly and rhythmically as she settled into a troubled, drug induced sleep. A rogue greying strand drooped across her ear and he took the time to place it carefully around her earlobe. He continued his gentle, loving caressing, the regular movement helped to focus his thoughts. Alison's breathing became less laboured as her tormented mind settled into an artificial deep sleep and once he was sure she would remain asleep he gently stroked her face, leant down and lovingly kissed her forehead, as if a father to a sleeping baby. He then stood up from his sitting position on the bed, reached out and took the Diazepam bottle from the bedside cabinet. He had this left-over drug from when his GP had prescribed them for anxiety attacks caused by his Post Traumatic Stress Disorder, a condition that he'd now learned to live with thanks to intensive psychology at

Royal Cornhill Hospital in Aberdeen. Reliving harrowing events from his army days with his therapist had been torturous, but now his brain was able to process them, store them correctly in his memory and allow him to move on with his life. He opened his bedside drawer and placed the pill bottle deep within its recesses.

Looking down at his sleeping wife he nodded once, patted her hand as if making his mind up about a difficult decision, and removed his dressing gown and pyjamas. He laid them carefully on his side of the bed so as not to disturb his wife and wasted no time in getting dressed. He looked back briefly at her still form as he left their bedroom, satisfied that her regular breathing demonstrated a deep, albeit a drug-induced, sleep. He gently closed the door and paused briefly outside his daughter's room. There was no sound, Bella could sleep through anything, like her father. He left the two surviving loves of his life and went to be with his son.

She had sat quietly in the dark room, with her curtains slightly ajar. The yellowish amber of the new bulbs in the streetlamps afforded her some night vision around her street. She had watched in puzzlement as the two young police officers had quickly made their way to their car. She had instinctively ducked as the younger of the two had looked in her direction when she had sprung up for a closer look, her hand automatically pulling the curtains together as she had been caught, like a nosey child sat at the foot of the stairs, peering through the slats of the bannister as the grown-ups argued. Through the even more narrowed opening she had watched as they pulled away and then was puzzled further as Hamish ran briskly to his car that had been parked close to the boundary wall. Her curiosity caused her to open the curtains a tad more, just in time to see him drive off with urgent haste. She pulled her nightgown closer over her bony frame and sat in vigil for developments.

The strobing blue lights of the three police cars and two ambulances lit up the night's countryside like a macabre disco as the bracken and trees danced to their silent song. Hamish pulled his foot from the accelerator and stamped on the brake. He had been speeding to get here and as he braked hard, he could make out the derelict farm buildings to his right, by the junction to the Aberdeen, Peterhead and Fraserburgh turn-offs. Their dilapidated bricks and caved in roof slates were illuminated in turns by the emergency lights of the vehicles. This was a notorious accident spot and his son would not be another statistic. By his side sat his medi-bag, stuffed full of life-saving equipment. He just had to reach Paul, and all would be right.

He could see the young police officer waving to him, her safety stripe on the sleeve of her jacket illuminated in the darkness, cautioning him to stop. Her police car had earlier been moved to allow another ambulance access, and she had omitted to pull her car back into the central part of the road as she'd been called over by the other ambulance crew to help retrieve the driver from the mangled car on the side of the road. His breathing had become laboured and he had to be pulled out quickly.

'STOP!' she was now warning the approaching car that must have driven through the diversion signs placed by her colleagues further up the road.

Hamish pretended to slow down and come to a halt in front of the officer. He slyly waited until the police officer drew alongside him, to the driver window. She had anticipated the driver unrolling his window to ask about the accident and then for alternative directions to Aberdeen. Instead Hamish shouted out a 'Sorry lass!' and slowly accelerated away, glancing in his side mirror to ensure he had not accidentally struck her with his car. He could see her running towards him, so he drove faster, all the while taking in the scenes of the accident.

He uttered several swear words as he saw how mangled the black car was and a feeling of relief swept over him like a calming massage as he knew this was not Paul's car. The officers who came to his house had gotten it wrong. Nevertheless, he could be of help he thought, so he parked up by the first ambulance and swiftly applied his handbrake and cut off the engine. He leant over and grabbed his first-aid kit holdall and exited his car as the female police officer gained on him. She grabbed him by the shoulders, surprising him into a twist that pushed him roughly against his car and that was when he saw them.

Various scarves of Aberdeen Football Club were fluttering on the floor, as if a fan was cheering on his team. Some of the scarves were twenty years old. They were from a collection, bought outside Pittodrie Stadium and saved over the years and handed down from father to son. He dropped his medical bag in despair as he looked above his car roof and further into the adjacent field. The strobing blue lights of the emergency services vehicles illuminated an upturned and crumpled red Volkswagen Golf. Nearby more football scarves fluttered in the wind, as if giving a wave of direction. The police officer pushed him hard into his own car, grabbed his wrists and pulled them behind his shoulders. It was then that he could make out a body in the field. It was lying askew in the mud, limbs akimbo as if pulled from their sockets and rearranged by a grisly puppet master. Hamish could make out the fair hair of his boy ruffling in the wind by an unseen hand and tried to look into his dead face, buried in the mud, but he was pulled away by the officer who, with surprising ease of experience had restrained his hands behind him with handcuffs, and shouted, 'WHAT ON EARTH DID YOU THINK YOU WERE DOING?'

Hamish twisted around violently, unintentionally knocking the petite woman sideways. She stumbled and tripped over his medical kitbag and her cry of surprise alerted two of her colleagues who came running over.

'THAT'S MY SON!' screamed out Hamish, spittle flying from his mouth and onto his car window. 'I NEED TO GET TO HIM, LET ME GO! GET ME OUT OF THESE HANDCUFFS. I CAN HELP HIM. I'M MEDICALLY TRAINED.'

The running of booted feet momentarily took Hamish back to his army days, his mind whirled and danced and conjured up an assortment of disturbing images until these unexpected memories were interrupted by two policemen holding him firmly by his shoulders. He cried out, softer and with deeper despair, 'Please. Let me go, I have to be by my son, I can save him.'

The two policemen kept their firm hold on him, but looked to each other, unsure of what to do. Their colleague regained her footing and stood up and walked over to the trio. She placed her hands onto the man's shoulders and nodded to her colleagues. They withdrew their holds. She then gently turned him around. 'Sir. Look at me.'

Hamish snapped out of his dark thoughts at the gentleness of her voice, as if hypnotised, but still able to repeat a mantra, 'That's my son,' he whimpered.

The police officer wrapped her arms around Hamish and held him close. She leant her lips to his ear and whispered, 'I'm so sorry Mr Dewart, we know that it is Paul, but he's gone. He's gone.' She looked down at the medi-bag with its strewn bandages, needles, syringes and bags of fluids and turned back to Hamish, released her hold and placed both hands gently on his shoulder and affirmed, 'The best doctor, medic or nurse in the world could not have saved your son. I'm afraid he died instantly. Please go home. You don't want to see your boy like this. Let us do our job. Remember him as he was. I'm going to release your handcuffs now.' She gently turned him around and unlocked the handcuffs. Hamish allowed himself to be turned and moved, resigned to his grief and loss, a willing participant to the play that was unfolding around him.

An ambulance technician came running over to the female police officer. As he reached her, he said, 'Thanks for your help earlier, my colleague is just settling him in the back. He'd have choked on his vomit if we hadn't gotten him out. He absolutely reeks of booze, God know how much he's had to drink.'

Hamish snapped out of his trance and yelled a guttural base scream as he shirked off the unlocked handcuffs and flung them off his wrists as he turned around and barged past the stunned police officers and ambulance technician. He ignored his first-aid kit, Paul was long gone, but now he could avenge him. He ran to the ambulance, the brightly lit interior was his goal, revenge was his motivation.

He sprinted like an Olympian, the police behind him trying to keep up. His muscles, unused to such long-forgotten speeds ached, and his chest cried out like an anguished soul at this sudden exertion. He somehow found the strength from deep within his aging body to power towards his goal. He reached the ambulance and ignored the steps and the side ramp and leapt up into the back to be nearer the drunk driver who had taken his son's life. He saw the other ambulance technician sensibly back away from this snarling madman who had burst into his safe workplace and upset its equilibrium. Hamish looked down at the blood-soaked face of the monster who had taken his son's life and advanced upon him with outstretched hands, ready to throttle the life out of the drink-addled fiend.

Four pairs of hands stopped him and working as one, partly lifted him and dragged him out of the ambulance. Hamish's feet were lugged down the two large and deep steps of the ambulance, the dull thuds of each foot echoed long into the night as he was hauled to the side of the vehicle. Each of the three police officers and ambulance technician looked to the other as they pinned this man against the side of the ambulance. They matched the man's heavy, laboured breathing, breath for breath for several moments. Then, once more, the female police officer took the initiative and intervened and breathlessly said in a quiet and sympathetic voice, 'There are some things that a father can be forgiven, isn't there lads?' as she looked to each of her colleagues in turn. All returned her comment with a solemn bow of agreement as they tried to catch their breath.

'Sir. Go home to your family,' stated the ambulanceman, panting away. 'They need you, I'm so sorry that we were too late for your lad, it was awful, but it would have been quick. I can assure you that he would not have suffered. Please let our colleagues care for him and do their job. Go home and none of us will report this.'

Hamish sagged, the anger expelled in the run and jump he had taken to reach the ambulance. An inner calm passed over him as he realised what he'd almost done, what he was surprised to find himself capable of. He really would have taken a man's life. 'I'm so sorry, I don't know what I was thinking,' he muttered crestfallen. He looked across to the field where his son lay. He could see white suited people setting up their bright arc lights whilst other uniformed police officers rolled out their yellow and black barricade lengths of tape. 'Please take care of my boy,' he sighed as he resigned himself to reluctantly leaving his son, 'please cover Paul with a blanket, he hated to be cold.'

Chapter 3

Tears silently fell from Hamish's eyes as he drove down towards his village. He blinked several times in a vain effort to clear his vision. As he rounded the corner, he could see the familiar shape of the lighthouse, whose flashing beam of light provided no comfort. Instead it acted as a warning, that perils were ahead, that his life had been caught in a storm and was about to be spun through a violently tossing sea and that he was in danger of drowning in his own grief. The flashing light strobed across the nearby skerry of rocks and failed to disturb the seagulls that were nestled there for the night, safe from predators.

Few lights were on in the rows of old fishermen's cottages as he steadily drove past them. Where once there would have been creels sat outside, awaiting transport to a fishing boat, there were now wheelie bins and pots of hardy plants. Hamish continued towards the more modern houses, where his wife and daughter slept. They were built from solid and dependable granite, cut from the nearby Kemnay Quarry. He sighed and drew strength from a deep inhalation. Like this quarried stone, he had to be the basis of foundation for his family. He must regroup, gather strength and be strong for them, be their rock. He slowed down as he reached his home. He could see the familiar climbing roses glasswork making their way up his front door, backlit by the hallway light. Normally he would smile at their beauty, but not tonight, perhaps not ever. Hamish struggled with his gears, his hands, and indeed his legs, still shaking from his earlier adrenaline-pumping run. He crunched the gears into reverse and carefully backed into the driveway that would now only need to accommodate one car.

He bit into his snack and relished the sharp, sugary taste of the chocolate as his tongue delved into the centre, seeking out more gooey delight, like a child licking an ice-cream at the beach promenade for the first time. He leaned back against the car's headrest as he relaxed into the seat, shut his eyes and let his shoulders sag as he contentedly exhaled and gave an appreciative 'mmm.' He continued eating the donut, enjoying every bite. His cup of hot chocolate was laid precariously on the dashboard as its heat steamed up a large circle of misty wetness onto the windscreen.

His colleague smiled and pressed the button to unwind his side window a fraction, despite the night's chilly air and now gentle spit of rain. *'It was like having his younger brother working alongside him. He wanted to teach him so much, but knew he'd learn better by doing and having to face the challenges himself, with guidance and prompting as needed. He even eats like my Nathan,'* he thought as he sipped his coffee and watched the windscreen slowly clear. The car park was empty. The boy racers had cleared off as they pulled into the drive-through and had placed their regular order through the intercom. The sleepy sounding assistant had even given them their ten-percent discount without having to see their Blue Light Card, a scheme that rewarded the 999 team with well-deserved generous offers. Looking over to his colleague he thought, *'He even puts the food away like him, hollow-legs, that's what their sister called him.'* He smiled as he thought how lovely it would be to be able to eat donuts and not worry about middle-aged spread. Then he frowned, *'Jesus, that poor sister, having to wake up to the news that her brother, her best friend, Paul had died.'* He did not envy Mr Dewart having to perform that paternal duty. *'What a mind melt.'*

His earpiece crackled and interrupted his dark thoughts as his colleague was busy licking his fingers clean of every morsel of sugar, his energy fix for his youthfulness satisfied. He put his finger to the radio piece so that he could hear above the noise of his young pal's eating habits. He breathed out long and hard, took an intake of breath and said, 'Jesus, you'll never believe what's just happened at one of the skyscrapers in Aberdeen? Fuck me, but I'm glad we aren't attending that shout.'

She peered around the window to see better, she was now sat on the edge of her armchair, which she had struggled to drag across to the first pane of glass. She was perilously close to falling off her seat as she looked on in puzzlement as Hamish returned, looking unusually wet from the comfort of his dry car. He looked absent from reality, almost as if he were sleep-walking. She had never known him to park in the middle of his driveway before. Surely, he hadn't left enough room for Paul to park when he returned home from work?

Hamish kicked off his shoes in the hallway which seemed so empty now that the two strapping policemen were no longer there. He absently rubbed his left shoulder, it still smarted after being thrown against the ambulance. '*Not that it mattered*,' he thought. He made his way into the lounge, switched on the lights, and was drawn to the smiling photograph of his son. His painful shoulder drooped, and he sluggishly made his way to the drink cabinet. He opened the fold-down compartment, reached in for his 12-year-old malt whisky and poured himself a double measure, his hands were visibly shaking, but none of the precious spirit was spilt as he placed his other hand on the glass to steady it. With trembling hands, he lifted the heavy-based tumbler and walked over to the fireplace. He looked longingly at his son's photo, as if willing it to come to life, to say that it was all a joke, that he truly was still alive. His heart sank again as the truth rose within his mind, like an uncoiling sinister snake, ever ready to pounce upon its prey. He raised up the tumbler of whisky and said with a heavy heart. 'here's to you son, I loved you like no other, my dear boy, Paul.' He took a long, much needed gulp of the spirit and then held it aloft to the spirit of his son. It remained untouched.

The white-suited figures wrestled with the tarpaulin sheet as it billowed in the wind like a wraith floating through a spiritual plain. The rain drizzled down as if to offer elemental support by driving the tent downwards. The forensic team won as they gently drove home the tent pegs that stabilised the fabric that offered them and their evidence refuge from the weather. They looked down at the smashed and disfigured corpse within the field with professional distance as one by one they went about clinically cataloguing and photographing so that a warm, dry Sheriff, the Scottish Judge of the Aberdeen Court, could clinically assess and sentence the drunk driver along with fifteen good men and women of the jury who would look in horror at the evidence laid before them.

Hamish climbed the stairs, as he had done for decades. Only this time he felt that the home they had made for themselves was now just a house. It had been drained of all fun, vitality and youthfulness. As he held the bannister he thought of all the times that Paul had run up and down these stairs, eager to play in his room, on his favourite computer games, with his online pals and those he'd brought back from school, college or work. The silence around him threatened to overwhelm him with outpourings of emotions and grief. He'd often complained, half-jokingly, that Paul had treated the place like a hotel, often only appearing for meals. Yet, his mother would probably yearn for this for many years to come. *'We all would,'* he silently thought grimly as he ascended the stairs, *'oh how I wish my laddie would just come home,'* he sighed helplessly as he looked at the framed pictures on the walls, all done by Bella and Paul at various ages as they grew up in this supposedly safe area. With all the hotspots that Hamish had been to in his army career, he wryly never thought that it would be one of his kids that perished. *'It was not natural for a father to see his dead son,'* he thought bitterly *'it should be the other way around.'* He climbed the final steps, impotent to his rage.

She looked down with disdain in her eyes at the half-naked overweight man on the stretcher as the ambulance technicians applied their suction tubes to his mouth to rid him of the latest bout of vomiting. The police officer resumed going through the personal effects, hoping to find some form of identification. The paramedics removed the sucker with a final '*slurp*' and reapplied the oxygen mask. Their vehicle stunk like the floor of a Belmont Street bar after freshers' week. They hoped that the drunk would keep the mask on this time and not wrench it off with flailing confused arms. The older of the two now reached across and pulled out a cannula set from one of their drawers and they nodded to each other in a well-rehearsed drill that had been performed countless times in their ambulance.

She felt along the inner pocket of his black suit and found what she had been looking for and pulled out the faded brown leather wallet. There, amongst a good wad of tenners, was the driving licence that she had hoped to find. As she silently read to see who this drunk was, she let out an unexpected, 'Oh shit!' which caused the paramedic to miss the big purple vein that his partner had so expertly tempted out with the tourniquet and gentle tapping on skin. They silently tutted as they undid the tourniquet and looked across in hope to the other arm of the now snoring inebriate as the oxygen gently lulled his lungs to sleep.

'Is that you love?' cried out a sleepy Alison, the Diazepam making her slur and mumble her words.

Hamish pushed their bedroom door closed, the familiar movement was well-rehearsed in his muscle memory, and he automatically did it as quietly as possible. 'Aye love, it is that, you try and get back to sleep lass,' he replied quietly with a weariness that was unfamiliar to him. It was not just physical, nor was it through lack of sleep, but it was a deeply emotional exhaustion. He stood in the dark room, waiting for his night vision to help orientate him around the room. He wanted his wife to sleep for the few hours before their daughter Bella would awaken at the second time her mobile phone alarm went off.

'I had the most awful nightmare Hamish. I dreamt that Paul had died.' She gave a small whimper in her sleep and then started a gentle snoring pattern that did nothing to help soothe Hamish's troubled mind.

'I'm so sorry lass,' he gently muttered, 'our living nightmare has only just started, and I can't protect you from it.' He sighed as he moved over to his side of the bed as quietly as his bulky shape could. Stretching over the bed, he ever so gently took hold of some of the duvet and pulled it more to his wife, so that if she rolled over there would be spare material to follow her. He stroked her hair and then stopped and clasped her cheek with such tenderness. She remained sleeping on her side. Without removing any of his wet clothes, he softly laid down next to his wife, on top of the duvet and lovingly took her in his arms, his profound love for her penetrating deeply through the high-togged duvet. Only when his mouth and nose were smothered right into the bedding, to stifle all sounds, did he then release his torrent of tears and mental anguish, long into the night.

Bella's mobile-phone alarm jingled and vibrated on her bedside cabinet. Its sound and movement growing more insistent with each passing second. A small sleepy hand unfurled itself from the depths of her duvet and reluctantly braved the cold of the winter's morning to turn it to snooze mode. Her hand shot back into the warmth and she, like many teenagers before her, turned over and instantly fell back asleep, all thoughts of needing to be up to catch the College bus long forgotten, for ten minutes at least.

Upon hearing the distant sounds of his daughter's alarm Hamish withdrew his arms from around his wife and with his hands he quickly dried his tears from around his eyes, cheeks and down his neck. He then sat up and reached over to his bedside cabinet and withdrew a couple of tissues from a box and blew his nose, sounding like a foghorn alerting sailors to the deadly rocks nearby. He bunched them up and threw them into the wicker basket in the corner. He then stood up, found his bearings, and took several deep breaths to ensure that his voice would be steady. He walked around the bed, each step feeling like a long walk down a never-ending corridor. He sat down by his wife's side and gently said her name, 'Alison, love, you need to get up now.'

Alison mumbled incoherently in her drug-addled haze. Hamish gently shook her. She opened her eyes and gave them a rub, to free the grit that always seemed to gather in the crooks, like dirt in a corner of a bedroom carpet. She looked straight into Hamish's eyes, panic was in hers as she struggled to breathe and speak at the same time.

'Paul's gone!' she exclaimed to her husband as he reached around her and gathered her towards his large, but reassuring frame. He held her close as he rocked her and whispered shushing noises.

'I know lass, I know,' he sighed. 'We have to be strong now, for Bella.' He withdrew his embrace and looked at her, trying to convey his love. He started nodding and was pleased that she was nodding too.

'But our son, Hamish, he's gone, our lovely, beautiful boy,' she cried out as tears ran down her face. She fell back into his embrace and sobbed deeply into his shoulder, for the son she had carried for nine months and for the baby she had nurtured and cared for and for the toddler she had comforted, taught, and had fun with. Tears fell like the heaviest rainfall, but these would not cleanse away her raw, emotional pain as she thought of their child who turned into the handsome, but stroppy teenager who had then blossomed into a thoughtful and caring young man. Now horribly snatched away from her tender heart. She knew that it would be a long time before she felt any joy once more. Perhaps she never would.

She felt the comforting pat on her shoulder, Hamish's way of saying *'that's enough now lass.'*

'Oh Hamish,' she sighed as her shoulders shuddered at the enormity of this life-changing event. 'Oh Paul, my dear Paul,' she whimpered as tears cascaded down her cheeks once more.

'I know lass, I know,' said Hamish as he thought, only us two could truly know. He held his wife tighter and sat quietly and still as she cried for their son. Her tears mingled with his, in a loving, but distraught union.

Chapter 4

The downstairs bathroom door closed as a new, dark and lonely chapter dawned on Bella's life. Unawares of this change to come of her sibling friendship, she got on with her morning toilet habits whilst upstairs, her parents were composing themselves to bring her the most shocking of news. Their hearts would be broken once more.

'Here lass, put this on,' ushered Hamish as he handed Alison her dressing gown. He expertly guided her arms through its sleeves, an action he had done for countless patients in his charge over the years. He moved around her and drew in the excess material and tightened its belt. He then placed his hands gently on each of her cheeks, looked long into her tearful, reddened eyes, and said, 'Okay lass, be brave for our Bella.'

Alison started sobbing and between tears she cried out, 'Oh Hamish, I don't think I can.'

Hamish drew her closer and said, 'Yes love, yes you can. I know you. I've seen you endure hours of labour, twice. Then deliver two mighty bundles of fun. Oh, such love we had for them. Even though you were so tired, you nurtured them and took them to your breast and nursed them. You took to motherhood like a duck to water. I have seen you be there for each of them, when they took their first steps, had to wave me goodbye as I went overseas on dangerous postings, had exam anguish, and fell out with their first boyfriend and girlfriend. And now you will be there for Bella. She needs her mother. And I will be there for you, my love, for both of you.'

Alison dried her eyes, drew up straight and said, 'Aye Hamish, aye.' Though she thought, *'and who will be there for you?'*

Alison took hold of Hamish's hand as they walked out of their bedroom. She patted it twice as they reached the landing and Hamish acknowledged this and took the lead down the stairs. When they both reached the lounge, they instinctively held hands again. Hamish gave hers a small squeeze of comfort as the bathroom door opened and Bella happily stepped out, carrying her phone at eye-level, watching a television programme, as she made her way to the kitchen. She did a double-take at seeing her parents and walked back to the doorway of the lounge. 'What are you two doing up so early, are you making me breakfast?' She looked at the posture of her parents, it had been years since she'd last seen them hold hands. 'Why so glum?' she asked as she hit the pause button on her phone and slipped it into her jeans pocket.

'Bella,' mumbled Hamish, finding the words for destroying his daughter's life difficult to form, 'come here lass,' he managed to ask.

'What, what's going on?' questioned Bella as she hesitantly moved forward, not wanting to enter their world. Her instincts told her that something was awry and was about to shatter her cosy world.

Her father held out his free hand, encouraging his daughter to step further forward. She took his hand, still huge compared to hers, usually reassuringly huge, but not now. Her mother moved forwards and grasped her free hand. 'There is no easy way to say this Bella…' began Hamish, floundering at telling his daughter the news he had so easily told others in the past, during his time as a nurse in the army and then in the nursing homes or on the NHS wards at Aberdeen Royal Infirmary.

'Oh no!' cried out Bella. 'It's Paul isn't it, where is he?'
She looked around the room, praying that he'd be sat in the
corner armchair. She broke off their grips and ran from the
room, wailing as she went first into the kitchen, then
through to the conservatory. Doors were flung open in her
haste to find her brother. As she ran, she was unaware that
her mobile phone had worked loose from her pocket and
had dropped to the floor. Her fruitless search saw her run
back through the ground floor rooms and then sprint up the
stairs, a childlike scream following her as it echoed
heartlessly around the house, deafening her parent's ears
with such heart-wrenching sorrow. They heard her
pattering feet move from bedroom to bedroom, doors
thundering open as their beloved daughter's movements
proved futile. Bella ran down the stairs, shouting out
Paul's name. She burst into the lounge. She threw her arms
around her parents and the trio moved as one, into an

embrace of grief as they knew they would no longer be a quartet.

'I'm so sorry Bella, Paul was killed in a car accident in the early hours,' said her dad, now believing the words himself, no longer in shocked denial. He held her tight as she howled into her mother's shoulder, digging deep into her flesh as if to climb back into the safety of her womb. Only no comfort could be had, not now, and not for a long time.

Chapter 5

She paced her lounge, fretting with each moment as dawn slowly rose and the winter's light half-heartedly peaked up and then paused, as if not wanting to intrude on the grief playing out next door. She had heard the desperate running of feet and the slamming of doors through the thin walls and then the blood-curdling scream that froze her like a walk-in freezer at the butchers. '*Oh Lord, please don't let it be what I think it to be,*' she prayed and bargained. '*Not that, they don't deserve that.*' She gave up her vigil by the window, his red car had not come home, it wasn't parked where it should be. She rose and attempted to stretch to her full height, or as much as her spinal curvature from her osteoporosis would allow. Stiff with waiting, she hobbled off to get dressed.

Bella dried her eyes with the tissue that her mum had given her. She flopped down onto the sofa and let out a large sigh, as if trying to expel the sad news. She leaned forward and put her head into her hands and started crying again. Her parents sat down either side of her and put their arms around her, cuddling into her as if they could reach into her soul and take away her anguish. 'What happened?' she asked into the room as she slowly sat up to reveal her grief-stricken features.

'Paul's car landed in a field and he was thrown from it during the crash. It would have been quick,' answered her father as he took her hands in his.

Bella cried more, now in shock, not wanting to hear the news, but accepting it anyway. Her parents had never lied to her and were too old to start doing so now.

Alison looked up, puzzled, 'I thought I felt you leave the room last night Hamish, did you go to the crash site in the early hours. It's all a bit foggy.'

Bella, stunned out of her crying, looked across. Her mother saw her quizzical look and realised what she was thinking. 'I only slept because your dad gave me one of his calming pills. The night was a bit hazy, I'm not used to such heavy sedatives.' Mother and daughter looked to Hamish.

'I had to, sorry.' He looked down to the carpet, where several hours before two policemen had looked down as he cried. 'I thought that my medical skills might save him, but they couldn't. We've lost your brother, our son, and nothing I could have done would have saved him.' Hamish looked up from the carpet, gazed into his daughter's tear-stained face and burst out crying. It was now Bella's turn to comfort her father in a macabre game of pass the grief parcel as all of Paul's loved ones took turns to cry out for his return and the injustice that he had died so young.

The house telephone rang out, snapping the trio out of their emotional embrace. Hamish stood up, 'I'll get it,' he said as he walked to the table. He passed Paul's photograph once more and his son beamed down, as if to say, '*that'll be about me.*'

'Hello,' Hamish tersely stated, as if angry at this tenderly touching family time being rudely interrupted.

'Er, hello, Mr Dewart?' asked a breathless voice.

'Yes. It is,' briefly stated Hamish.

'Hello Mr Dewart,' continued the breathless voice, 'my name is Catriona, I'm your dedicated police liaison officer. Let me begin by saying how sorry I was to hear of your son's passing.'

Hamish hesitated as he walked through to the kitchen with the cordless phone. 'Thank you, only he didn't simply pass away, did he?'

'Er, no. Yes indeed, Paul had a car accident...'

'No. That's not what happened, is it? I went there. I saw how it really was for myself.'

'Ah, yes,' replied Catriona, her breath now all but caught up. 'I heard about that, most unusual.'

'Please don't sugar-coat anything Catriona, Paul deserves better than that. A drunk driver shunted him off the road, that's what it looked like to me.'

'I'm so sorry for your loss Mr Dewart, but we don't have the facts yet.'

'Please don't lie Catriona, we deserve that much. I've just had to tell my daughter that her brother won't be coming home, she, as we all are, is heartbroken.'

'So sorry Mr Dewart, I appreciate that this is not an easy time for you, and your family. That's why a blind eye is being turned to last night's, er, odd activities. Yes, it does seem like that is what happened, but we do have to wait for official channels to state these things. Please be assured that a thorough investigation is under way.'

'Has he been arrested and charged?'

'I can confirm that a male was indeed charged and is in custody, relating to your son's death. The reason for my call is to ask if a family member can come to the mortuary and formally identify that it is Paul. Could this be done this morning please, at your earliest convenience. I'm guessing that it will be you, Mr Dewart?'

'Yes. That is my duty,' replied Hamish as he looked up at the kitchen clock and was surprised to see that it was 9am already. 'I must inform my parents before they learn of Paul's death from the local press.' He thought about all the times he had seen photographs in the local newspaper or live video on local television news channels of crumpled up cars. '*They shouldn't be allowed to do that,*' he thought bitterly, '*have they no shame, can they not see the damage that could do to grieving relatives who might be imagining all sorts of injuries and what pain their loved one must have been in?*'

'Are you still there Mr Dewart?' asked a worried Catriona, unknowingly interrupting Hamish's chain of thought.

Hamish left a void to her silence whilst he thought some more. 'Yes, sorry lass, I was thinking. I will have to go via my parents, to break the bad news. Can we say about noon?'

Catriona sucked air through her teeth as she thought. 'There's been a double murder and suicide overnight, at the high-rises, but I think the lads in the mortuary can fit you in then.'

Hamish left a longer silence. Better manners were forcing him to stay quiet as he was silently angry at her for not giving his son top priority. He did not need to hear about other people's deaths. 'Thank you. I understand that Paul is now in Aberdeen, at your Queen Street morgue?'

'Yes, I'm afraid that's the nearest facility. Do your parents live nearby?'

'Yes, they are on the way,' replied Hamish as he darkly thought, *'as is where Paul lost his life, and it is the only route to Aberdeen. How do I dare take them past it?'*

This observation was lost on Catriona, who blissfully carried on. 'When you get to the police building, please go to the barrier at the car park and take a token from the machine. You'll need this to get out again. Then proceed to the main reception and ask for me. My surname is Foster. Once again, Mr Dewart, I'm so sorry for your loss.'

Hamish thanked her, and as he said goodbye and pressed the call end button, he grimly thought that he'd better start getting used to folk saying those words. His thoughts turned to his elderly parents and the anguish he was about to bring into their lives at such a vulnerable age. Thank heavens that he didn't speak to his brother and have his grief to cope with.

The doorbell rang, interrupting Hamish's thoughts. It was insistent upon its second and then third intrusive ring. Hamish thought of taking out its batteries, this was a time for family only. He walked reluctantly to the door.

As he opened it a draught of air flew in and caused the inner lobby door to fly open behind Hamish, though he had closed it tightly only seconds earlier. On his doorstep, wrapped up in a loosely worn jacket was his elderly neighbour, Molly. Her jacket was draped over her shoulders and not zippered up, as if she expected to take it off at any moment. As if in confirmation she took a step forward and tried to look beyond Hamish's broad shoulders, towards the kitchen and lounge of the neighbouring home. 'Hello Molly,' said Hamish flatly, as he reached out and took her aged hand.

Molly stopped bobbing up and down and back and forth like a rugby player preparing to breach a wall of opponents. 'Hello Hamish, is everything okay?' she asked, confused by the hand-holding. 'Only I saw the police car earlier and the two men came in here, then you left, a wee while after they left, then I heard lots of crying a bit later,' she blustered out, her words almost tripping over her tongue in their eagerness to get out.

Hamish patted her hand with his free hand, not releasing his gentle hold. 'Och, lass, it's bad news, really bad news,' he pushed open the outside door even more. 'Come away into the house Molly.'

Molly, fearing the worst, for she knew that the police don't wake you up in the middle of the night for no reason, turned pale as her worst horrors had been confirmed. She quickly wiped her feet and entered her neighbour's home just as Hamish was re-closing the inner lobby door. She shut the outside world away as she carefully closed the main front door. She and Hamish were now huddled close, like two passengers in a small lift, waiting to get out at their designated floor. Only this destination was misery, she could feel it oozing from Hamish, like a discrete sheen of perspiration.

Hamish took hold of both her hands now and said in a low voice, 'Poor Paul, he was in a car accident late last night, he died at the scene. I'm so sorry lass, there is no easy way to say it.'

Molly broke from Hamish's hand-holding and embraced him, she was enveloped up in his large frame as he reciprocated the hug, her frame delicately wrapped up in his as she wept. 'Oh Hamish,' she eventually managed to say.

'I know lass, I know. Paul was so full of life and he's been snatched away from us all.'

Molly thought back over the years, to when the couple had moved in, they had struck up a friendship, despite the age gap. She'd been so delighted for them when soon after they had announced that they were expecting a family. She'd offered and was thankful that it was accepted, to babysit at any-time. Her family had flown the nest, quite literally with oil jobs across the globe, though one son lived nearby with his grown-up family. She'd loved the company of baby Paul and then baby Bella, and had watched them grow with great pride, almost as much as Alison and Hamish had. Then when the children grew too old for babysitting, they would exchange news over the fence, or brother and sister would often pop in for a cup of tea and a piece of homemade cake, as did Alison and Hamish when their nursing shifts allowed. 'He's too young to go,' she simply said between sobs.

Hamish patted her shoulder, much like he had done earlier to his wife. Molly came out of her grieving reverie and sniffed deeply, 'And how are Bella and Alison, oh the poor lassies.' She broke off the embrace and looked up to Hamish, 'And you, how about you?'

'Shocked lass, we are all shocked. We just can't take it in. We all just keep crying and crying. I've to go and identify him soon, but first I must tell my parents.'

'Oh Hamish, I wish I could save you that pain,' she cuddled him once more and then asked, 'is there anything I can do?'

'I was hoping you'd say that Molly, could you please come away in and look after my girls?'

'Och, of course, you didn't need to ask,' she gave him a playful thump across his arm, 'let me start by making you some breakfast. I know you probably won't feel like eating, I know I didn't when my Bill passed away, but it's the best thing you can do. I'll pop through into the kitchen and switch the kettle on. Have you phoned your work and Bella's College?'

'Oh, no, I hadn't thought of that.'

'Well you just write the numbers down for me,' fussed Molly, happy to be of help to the man who had helped nurse her Bill in his last few days, 'and I'll sort that out.'

'Thank you, Molly,' whispered Hamish as tears fell down his cheek.

Molly reached up, a handkerchief plucked as if from magic from within her clothing and wiped away his tears. She then shrugged out of her jacket. 'Right, you hang this up for me and tell your girls that I'm making them tea and toast.' She opened the lobby door and walked through to the familiar kitchen, straight to the kettle and walked across to the tap and filled it up. She then checked the fridge, made a mental note to buy more milk and started pouring some into mugs. She reached across for the teapot and popped several teabags into it. From here on in, she declared to herself, this pot will be kept topped up as she anticipated the deluge of visitors that she had to cater for. She walked over to the backdoor, slid the chain off and pocketed the backdoor key. Then she could let herself in and out with biscuits, cake and sandwiches. Hearing that the kettle had boiled she walked back to it and filled the

teapot to the brim. 'I'll just let that brew for a few

seconds,' she said aloud to nobody. Only then did she

allow herself to go through to her girls.

Chapter 6

'You'll not be doing that on your own,' protested Alison, her tears all but dried up.

'No dad, you listen to mum, we'll all go together, as a family.'

'Och, but it's too much for you, let me just go by myself,' objected Hamish.

'We need to see him, don't we Bella?' overruled Alison who was pleased to see her daughter nodding vigorously, despite her tears.

'Och, but the mortuary isn't the nicest of places. Let me do this.'

'No place is good to see your dead son, and besides, I've been in plenty of those when I used to nurse in the hospitals, they are all the same, cold and clinical,' argued Alison.

'Aye, maybe, but not Bella.'

'Please dad, let me come too, I need to see Paul, I can't believe he's gone. I need to see him.'

Hamish looked to both women in his life, he'd always know when to back down and lose the fight whenever they took sides against his point of view, and this was another, much more dramatic, time. 'Okay, but I want you both to eat something first.'

Taking her cue, just outside the lounge, Molly rushed in and flung her arms around Bella and Alison. 'Oh, my dears, my loves, I'm so sorry to hear about Paul. He was such a lovely boy, the loveliest. It's not fair, is it?'

Alison and Bella nodded their agreement, the three of them crying their hearts out as Hamish watched helplessly. *'I guess I'd better get used to sharing grieving over Paul,'* he thought, *'he touched so many lives and had so many friends, how am I to cope with it all?'* He looked up to the picture of his son, who still beamed down, as if to say, *'You'll cope dad, you'll cope.'*

The three women broke off their embrace and Molly ordered them about, 'I've made tea in the kitchen, you all pop through and take a mug. Then sit down whilst I make you toast. I expect you all to eat at least two slices before I let you go out of this house.' Bella, Alison and Hamish trundled through to the kitchen. As Hamish passed her, he placed his hand on her shoulder and simply said, 'Bless you Molly.'

The police officer leant over with a long heartfelt sigh and slowly, tiredly undid his laces and casually kicked off his heavy well-worn boots into the corner of the lobby and stepped through into their hallway with a deflated sigh. He looked about him at their family photos and gave a silent prayer of thanks.

'Daddy, daddy!' yelled out his son as he went running up to him and draped his hands around his legs and held on tightly. He was blissfully unaware that his latest Lego model dug into his father's wearied legs. 'Did you catch lots of bad guys?'

'Yes!' shouted his dad, feigning energy that he knew he just did not have as he stooped over, lifted his son and embraced him.

'Leave off dad, that's a bit tight,' complained the boy. 'Even uncle Nathan doesn't hug that hard,' he protested. 'Mum tell him!'

His wife came through from the kitchen, recognised the look, and went to retrieve their son from his father's tight cuddle. 'Why don't you go through and watch Paw Patrol, it's just about to start and you don't want to miss it.'

'See you later daddy!' shouted his son as he wriggled free and ran off into the lounge to be entertained by his canine pals.

She reached out for his hand, gave it a tight squeeze, and led him into the kitchen for his real debriefing and listening ear.

'I'll just pop to the corner shop and get more milk, I expect that toast to be eaten and the tea to be drunk when I get back,' ordered Molly.

The trio, sat around the kitchen table, heads and shoulders stooped low, played with their toast and cupped their hands around steaming mugs of tea. Each was too lost in their own thoughts of Paul to eat or drink but had nodded their agreement to her commands.

Molly sighed at the pitiful sight and wished that she could take their pain away from them. She knew that ahead of them, they had a long, difficult path to walk. Though her Bill had been gone for four years this February, she still missed him. She had cried several times an hour for the first week, then after the funeral it lessened to maybe six or seven times a day. As days turned into weeks the crying decreased, but the heartache never went away. She missed her Bill with all her soul, but her faith helped her. She knew one day that she'd be reunited with him once more. But he had led a good long life, had a career, marriage, children, fun holidays, good hobbies and a long retirement. Paul was snatched away too young. Though she understood grief and had a first-hand account, she little understood the loss of a child. '*Poor Alison and Hamish,*' she thought, '*will they ever get over it?*' Hearing Alison's fresh tears as she shrugged on her jacket and went out into the January chill confirmed her thoughts that, '*No, she never would.*'

'That's not like you to buy two cartons of milk Molly,' said Isaac, looking down onto his counter. He picked them up to scan across his till.

'No, and I don't think this'll be my last trip across to see you today, nor for the next few days.'

'Oh,' beamed Isaac, 'do you have company, has one of your sons come back from overseas? I hear those roughnecks have quite the appetite.'

'I wish that were the case, Isaac,' she said thoughtfully. She ruminated for a few seconds and then made up her mind. 'Ah, well,' she decided, 'you might as well hear it from me first.'

'Oh,' replied Isaac with a look of concern. 'Has something happened?'

'Yes. Oh, dear me, yes. Poor Paul has died, he was killed in a car accident late last night.'

'Oh my!' exclaimed Isaac. 'Not Hamish's and Alison's Paul?'

'Yes, I'm afraid so.'

'Oh dear, oh dear,' sighed Isaac as he thought of when young Paul would spend ages picking his comic from the display over to his left and then count out his pocket money to see what sweets he could buy. He still went on to buy sweets most days from his shop, though his comics gave way to car magazines. 'Oh, the poor boy, the poor parents. And Bella, to lose a brother at such a young age, that's not right. I must go over and pay my respects when Sarah comes on shift.'

'That's what the milk is for, it's the least I can do after they helped me with Bill. I'm making sure they and their guests are cared for.'

Isaac beamed down at her, 'They are blessed to have such a good neighbour.' He walked across to the other counter, raised the wooden section and walked through to the biscuit aisle. He randomly selected several packets of biscuits and walked back to his till and popped them, unscanned, into a plastic bag. 'Here, put your purse away Molly, these are on the house. And you make sure and come back and get some loaves and fillings. I'll tell Sarah to expect you and not to charge you. I'd help carry these, but I'm on my own in the shop.' He looked over to his CCTV system and from its screen he could see a customer by the nearby tinned soup section. This elderly woman seemed to be taking her time choosing a flavour from his small selection.

'Do you know what caused the accident yet?'

'Well, I'm not one to gossip,' said Molly as she took a step nearer to the till and conspiratorially continued, 'but I did overhear Alison tell Bella that the other driver had been drinking.'

'Oh my!' exclaimed Isaac, 'so the other driver is to blame?'

'That's right, but I don't think they'd want anyone to know, not just yet. Maybe after the police have confirmed it.'

They looked up as the shop door made its customary buzz as an elderly pair of legs made off without choosing her lunchtime soup, she had friends in the village to visit and gossip to share.

Chapter 7

Hamish sighed as he pulled his car up outside his parent's bungalow. He was grateful that his wife and daughter were with him. It was never easy breaking bad news, and he'd never had to do it to his own family. '*Well, until today, that is,*' he thought bitterly.

Alison leaned forward from her car seat and looked to his parent's window. 'It looks like they are in. We'll come in with you,' she insisted. She reached over and placed her hand onto his to demonstrate that she was there for him.

Hamish nodded his agreement, patted her hand and then he got out of the car and looked across to the wooded area in front of their home. He watched as the crows squawked and fought each other for dominance of the strongest branches. The sky behind them was still dark, matching his mood and emotion. He was about to bring more gloom into other lives. This dark January day seemed to stretch out before him. He reached down and opened the passenger door and said, 'C'mon love,' to his daughter, not wanting her to be left alone to her dark thoughts.

As they walked up the path, the door was opened by an elderly woman who was leaning on the doorframe, as if to take the weight off her unsupportive legs. 'This is a pleasant surprise. Grandfather's just popped the kettle on, come away in and get comfy.'

She allowed them to shuffle past her as they made their way into their grandmother's lounge. She stopped her son with a surprisingly strong grip to his arm, 'You've not lost your job, have you son?' she questioned.

'No mum, no. It's far, far worse than that.'

'I know it to be bad news, you don't often all come to see me during the day. You a day off then?' She looked back to her son's car. 'And where is Paul?'

Hamish closed the door to his parent's bungalow and took his mum by the arm, 'Come and sit yourself down mum.'

She allowed herself to be led by her son, grateful for the physical support. He led her to her favourite armchair, a riser and recliner that was already in the high risen position. She plopped herself down, gave a duck-like wiggle and pressed a button to move the chair to a normal sitting position. She looked ashen, and not just from the exertion.

'And how is everybody?' asked their grandfather and father as he walked through, drying his hands on a tea towel. He looked around, expecting to see his grandson. He threw the tea towel over his shoulder, as if he were a bartender in an American sitcom. He looked around him, at the ashen faces, and knew that this was not a comical day.

'Not well at all dad,' answered Hamish, suddenly crestfallen. He was about to break their hearts. He found himself repeating a well-worn phrase that he'd used several times already that morning, 'There is no easy way to tell you…'

'Spit it out son,' interrupted his father as he took down the tea towel and continued to dry his hands out of habit, though they were clearly dried.

'Paul was killed late last night, in a car accident. It looked to me like he'd been shunted from behind and forced off the road.

His mum gave a gasp of shock and Bella went over and sat on the arm of her chair and cuddled her grandmother close as they both wept.

Hamish's father continued to dry his hands, finding comfort in the familiar action. Tears were welling in his eyes and Hamish couldn't help but marvel at his stoicism. He had never seen his father cry before.

'After the police told us, I went to the crash site, I had to see Paul. But they wouldn't let me near him. I could see him though. He has gone. We've to be at the mortuary at noon to identify him.'

Hamish's mother continued to cry as Hamish's father said, 'I'll make that tea,' and left the room. Hamish knew, like he had earlier in the morning, that he'd gone to be on his own to cry. He left him a respectful few minutes.

Isaac took out an empty crisp box from the storeroom and walked back through to his small shop. He wandered around his shelves, thoughtfully placing biscuits, boxes of cups of soup and, ironically, he thought, large family-sized tins of soup into it, along with a large box of tea bags and a jar of coffee. He looked around for Sarah and sighed.

'*Sarah is better with the profit and loss, but this was not a time for thinking of money,*' he thought as he popped a box of tissues into the full box. He carried it back to his till area just as his wife walked into the shop from her early morning errands. She spied the box and the sullen look of her husband.

'Oh no!' she exclaimed as she saw the familiar range of contents, 'who?'

Hamish walked through to the kitchen to find his father drying his eyes with the tea towel. He looked down to the floor as he averted his eyes to the last of his father's fallen tears. He was a proud old man who rarely yielded to his emotions.

'Would it have been quick son?' begged his father, rubbing his hands now.

Hamish took the tea towel from him, popped it onto the nearest kitchen worktop and said, 'Aye father, aye. Don't tell the lassies, but yes, I could see Paul for myself. He would have had a momentarily bit of pain, but then instant death.' He broke down crying, hearing these words spoken out aloud by himself for the first time. He reached out for his dad and fell into his fatherly embrace.

'Oh son, you leave everything to me, I'll help with the funeral and take care of everything.'

Hamish, too emotional to say anything, merely nodded, grateful to release this burden from his pained shoulders.

'I'll get Cameron to help, it's time you two made up.'

Hamish pushed his father away, as if a bolt of lightning had been struck between them. He stood up straight and appeared to tower over his father, 'You'll do no such thing! You keep that monster away from my children. I've protected them for years from that paedo, and he'll get

102

nowhere near my Bella, do you hear old man? I've never known why you favoured him above me? After what he did!'

Hamish's father backed away, picking up the tea towel and turning it over and over in his hands like a comforter. He merely nodded to his son.

Hamish turned around and walked briskly out of his parent's kitchen and into the lounge, 'C'mon you two, we'll be late. Go to the car.' Without turning around or losing step, Hamish exited the bungalow and strode off to the car.

Bella looked to her mother. She shrugged as if to say, *'I don't know what that was all about.'* Both rose up numbly and Bella turned to her grandmother who remained seated and puzzled. 'I'll see you soon grandmother, we'd better stay with dad, we don't want him having to go through identifying Paul on his own.'

Still puzzled and stunned, her grandmother merely nodded and wondered at what had been going on in her kitchen, though she had her suspicions.

Sarah looked at the box, roughly calculating in her head the prices. *'I think we can cover those costs,'* she thought as she worked out their humble profits for this month. *'We'll mark them down as theft,'* she surmised as she thought of their tightly budgeted expense sheet, *'goodness knows enough goes on when their backs are turned. It'll be good to pay back the honest folk who have shopped here for years. Poor Paul and his family,'* she wistfully thought as she absently toyed with the tins and boxes within.

Looking for a nearby parking place, Hamish pulled over, appropriately enough, to the village's cemetery gates. He looked pensively over to the rows of headstones, not neat and in order like those in Belgium, in the care of the Commonwealth War Graves Commission. Those were of equal spacing and the headstones the same dimensions. These were of all shapes and sizes, ranging from large tombstones to small heart-shaped ones. He wondered which type they would choose for Paul, or would Alison prefer him to be cremated? It wasn't something he knew, nor something they would have discussed with him. Nor was it something they would have expected to have discussed as a couple for their first-born child. They'd never have imagined when they had held him as an infant, with that lovely baby smell ever-present in the air, that they'd have had to make this difficult decision one day.

'You okay dad?' asked a worried Bella who nervously fingered her beanie hat that lay in her lap.

'Yep,' replied Hamish immediately snapping out of his dark thoughts. He didn't want Bella to be worrying about him on top of everything else.

'Sorry about back there,' he said as he turned around. 'We've tried to protect you from it all, but now it's time to tell you.'

Alison unbuckled her seatbelt and exited the car without a word. She knew what was coming and swiftly walked to the passenger door and opened it. 'You wiggle across love, make some room for your mother.'

Bella obliged by undoing her seatbelt and stretched her legs over and followed through with her body to sit in the seat behind the driver, her dad.

Alison sat down and patted the middle-seated area. 'C'mon love, sit here. I need a cuddle.'

Bella smiled, though there was no warmth on her lips or eyes. She had a worried expression, anxious over what news was about to be delivered. 'Is it something else about Paul, the way he died. I don't think I want to know. I've never seen a dead body before mum.' She bit her trembling lip, she was on the verge of fresh tears again.

Her mum instinctively reached over and drew her daughter to her chest, as if about to breast-feed, a muscular memory from over eighteen years ago. She held her tight whilst kissing her head. She gave a small sniff and despite the day, laughed. 'Oh, I used to love smelling your two's hair all the time. First thing in the morning when I gathered you out of your cots, straight after your bath with the lovely smell of baby shampoo, through the night when I fed you, oh, you two…'

She left the sentence hanging in mid-air not knowing if she could ever again refer to her children in the plural, would it have to be child from now on? She burst into fresh tears and now it was the turn of the mother to seek solace from her daughter as she clung to Bella in the back seat.

'Maybe we'll save this for later,' said Hamish, taking command of the situation. It was his turn to exit the car. He walked over to the passenger door that his wife had left open and poked his head in, reached in further and then gave a comforting shoulder rub to his girls. 'Away and put your seatbelts on when you are ready, then we'll drive off and see our Paul.'

Chapter 8

The grey granite three-story building loomed before them, tucked up in the back streets of Aberdeen. It was located behind the hustle and bustle of the shops and bus stops of King Street and Union Street, appropriately enough, behind the Sheriff's Court. The 1960s architecture looked incongruously out-of-date, the once polished stone-work was now grimy and unwelcoming. Like a dark tower set amongst cliffs. Within its bowels lay a much-loved and already missed Paul.

Hamish had pulled up outside the nearby department store that had survived numerous recessions by mainly providing working attire for the ever-declining oil and fishing industry and for welcoming the patter of tiny feet as they went through growth spurts for brownie, cub, scout, boys brigade, guiding and various school uniforms.

Its welcoming window display was an easy distraction for the family who would no longer need any more clothing for a son, nor for his future offspring. The line of the Dewart family name was ended, and the building opposite would give them physical proof of that. Bella's future marriage would be the final removal of this line of descendance.

'You both could go into the store and get a cup of tea in the café whilst I go and see Paul and sign the paperwork for the police?' He left the question hanging. He wanted to cling tight to his girls and never let them go. Nor did he want them out of his sight. Not even for this important paternal duty.

'No.' replied a now composed Bella. 'I need to see Paul. I won't believe that he is gone until I see him for myself. I want to give him one last hug.'

'Oh lass, that's really brave of you. It'll look like he's just asleep. The staff there will make him look nice, won't they Hamish?' questioned Alison for positive reinforcement. Their marriage had been one of equality, one always backing the other's decisions. And to their credit, their children had never asked the other parent when one had already said no.

Hamish thought back to his army days, of the times that he had to handle, no carry, often man-handle, corpses onto stretchers and take them to non-descript buildings like this, often after a lonely solemn drive in an ambulance and on two occasions, by chopper. Then he would set to work washing away blood, mud, faeces and urine, all to make the body fit for loved ones to see. To pay their respects, hold and weep over. Now it was his turn to allow others to wash the field's mud off his son. To remove glass and metal that would inevitably be protruding from around his face and body. Or even to suture back on…He shuddered

at the distant memory of that incident and shoved it back

into the darkest recesses of his mind as he returned to the

role in hand, 'Aye lass. He'll look like he's fallen asleep

on the sofa, watching TV after a long shift. We'll be there

for you. You okay?' He asked, though he knew today

would not be an okay day for any of them.

'Yes dad, we'll go together and see if it is Paul.'

Hamish grimly turned the ignition key and pulled out

slowly to travel the few metres down the road to the

barrier, that led to the building where his son was soon to

be dissected and analysed. He pushed this darker thought

further from his mind and buried it with his other demons.

Catriona pulled back the sheet and gasped through gritted

teeth. She gave a low whistling air of harmony that danced

around the white-tiled room and cavorted with the objects

within the specimen jars. She breathed in that clinical-disinfectant type of air that was mingled with pavement and blood bone smells. 'Fuck me!' she involuntary exclaimed, 'That's, that's,' she struggled to say as she dry-heaved over the sheet that she had peeled back.

'That's the wrong cadaver, you want the one over there,' pointed the young man wearing the blue scrubs that contrasted sharply with his wiry and straggly beard that pushed for placement within his many facial piercings. He played with his tongue piercing and tickled his inner lips metalwork and studs as he struggled to contain a mischievous grin. 'That's the murderer who took a running jump off the flats. He's gross, isn't he? Fresh in. Don't be sick over him though. I thought you were getting used to this job now. You must have seen some sights as a police officer?'

'Yes, well, yes,' grappled Catriona with her words and her dry-heaving as she quickly threw the sheet back over the mangled corpse and tried to gather in some air from a fresher source. 'Okay,' she said in a higher pitch than she wanted. 'So, this'll be Paul? Poor lad,' she replied, pointing to the adjacent trolley that was parked in front of the three-layered high fridge doors that seemed to stretch forever along the wall.

The mortuary assistant smiled gloomily, 'yes, poor sod. I heard it was a drunk-driver and this poor guy was just an innocent driver that got in his way.'

'Yes, unofficially, of course. You heard about the father?'

'Oh yes. The whole department and probably the whole beat of the Shire knows about the father. I don't blame him. I'd have done time for the drunk if I'd had been there.'

'So, I'll put Paul in the viewing room, it's just the father coming, I think. Though given his desire to see his son, we'd better make sure we are locked up tight here. We don't want him tampering with the evidence before the post-mortem. That drunk deserves all that is coming to him. I hope they nail the bastard. You know who he is?'

'Oh yes!' cheered the assistant. 'It's about time that greedy fucker got put behind bars. Don't you worry. We are processing Paul by the book.'

Catriona walked over to the other trolley and carefully pulled back the sheet. She had heard that the shots to the two victims were to their faces. No wonder there had been so many ashen faces this morning. The bacon rolls and ketchup in the canteen had gone unbought this morning. She looked down and was pleasantly surprised to see the relatively unscathed face of Paul. There were just a few scratches and puncture wounds, mainly to his right side.

She would use viewing room one, that way she could position his left side nearer to the glass to hide most of his wounds from the windscreen he had shattered into and through. How his airbag hadn't deployed would be a job for the forensics to answer. She pulled the sheet back further and nodded in satisfaction that the assistant had already ensured that Paul's hands wouldn't fall off the trolley whilst it was being moved by placing the restraints in place. She flicked off the trolley brakes with a well-practised flick of her toes and pushed Paul on the start of his journey through the evidence system. '*This job doesn't get any easier,*' she thought. She'd transferred to the police liaison officer role just before Christmas because she didn't like the things she had to do and see as a beat officer. She hadn't realised just how grim this new position would be. She felt a knot in her stomach from knowing that the worst news ever would be clearly on display to the most disbelieving of eyes.

Irvine threw down his tablet in disgust. It bounced off the leather sofa, screen uppermost, and fell harmlessly onto the thick-carpeted floor. His father looked up from his newspaper with a disapproving look. 'For fuck's sake!' shouted Irvine.

'What! What's wrong son?'

'They shouldn't be allowed,' exclaimed Irvine as he paced the floor. He stormed back to the sofa and picked up his jacket and began rummaging about in his pockets.

'What is it?' asked his dad, more urgency in his question as he saw just how agitated his son was becoming.

Irvine picked up the tablet, 'the bloody local rag. It's their Facebook page. There's a photo of a police scene with a crumpled car, it looks just like Paul's. Where's my bloody phone?' he asked of the now anxiety-ridden room. The tension crackled in the air like an electric arc until it was discharged by his father saying. 'there, on the table. Let me look at that photo.' He took the tablet from his son with urgent hands.

'Jesus! That's terrible reporting right enough, blooming shocking picture. You wouldn't want to see that if you were the family.'

He looked to his son. 'Oh no! It can't be, can it?' One look at his son's pale face told him that unfortunately it was true. 'Not your Bella's Paul? Surely not?'

Irvine rapidly hit the contacts button and scrolled down for Bella's number. He rang it, but it dialled out.

The token sprang out like the coin reward at a noisy, flashing seaside amusement arcade, only this was no highly regarded prize. Hamish sighed as he reached across

118

from his car seat and plucked it from its metal hold. He wriggled and placed it in his trouser pocket then drove on into the nearest parking bay that was marked for visitors. His handbrake groaned and spoke aloud the inner-feelings of the trio. Then there was silence as they each composed themselves for their duty to their son and brother. 'Well girls, let's go and see our Paul,' whispered Hamish, resigned, into the rear-view mirror. They each simultaneously opened their car doors and exited as a family unit, albeit a recently broken up one.

Hamish pointed to the ramped area and they walked, downcast, like solemn mourners at a funeral, walking behind the coffin. CCTV cameras watched silently as they made their way to the glass doors. A few spatters of rain fell, as if the last tears of a dying man. The glass doors opened automatically, and they were met by a glass domed reception area, guarded against the grief that had descended upon the police headquarters. Hamish walked up to the grill area where secret conversations could be had between the stern looking receptionist and the common public. 'Hello. I'm Mr Hamish Dewart, my son was brought in. He was kil...' words failed Hamish as he struggled to acknowledge once more the reality of his ghastly situation.

Alison took him by the shoulders and gave him a squeeze, their covert sign for 'Don't worry, I've got this.' She drew herself up from her hunched grieved position. 'We've come to identify Paul Dewart, we are his parents and sister,' she said, forthrightly.

'Please take a seat,' ordered the prim receptionist. Her hair was tied up, giving her the appearance of a cheap facelift, which just made her look all the sterner. She pointed over to the grey metal framed chairs that had been bolted to the floor. *'Clearly unpleasant things had happened here with the furniture*,' thought Bella as she guided her father to the seats. She'd never been inside a police station before and did not know what to expect. She sat him down and held her father's hand whilst he composed himself once more.

The trio looked across to the receptionist who was speaking into a telephone. 'You've time to use the toilet Bella,' said Alison, pointing to a door that had the disabled, male and female bathroom signs.

'I think I will mum, Molly made me drink more tea than I'm used to.' She reluctantly let go of her father's hand for she had been drawing comfort from its large presence. She then stood up tentatively and then walked nervously over to the toilet, opened the door, peeked in and was relieved to see that there was only one cubicle beyond the sink. She locked the door and set about her business.

'Do you think I should go in first Hamish? You know, to make sure that Paul is presentable for Bella. You know what I'm saying, aye?'

'Aye lass,' replied a now composed Hamish. 'But it should be my duty, as his father.'

'We'll do it together, like we've always done for them.' She gave her husband's hand a squeeze.

'I'm just so glad that I was there for you when they were born. I'm so glad that I got time off for their births and wasn't half way around the world on a posting. I wouldn't have missed that for anything.'

Alison squeezed his hand again, 'You were a great father and still are. He'll always be our Paul,' she replied as tears flowed down her cheeks.

Hamish reached across and wiped her damp cheeks and then took his wife's face in his heavily-calloused hands.

'You're my bonnie lass, I love you, now be brave for our Bella.'

She reached into her pocket and drew out an already wet tissue and used it to dry her cheeks, eyes and then to blow her nose. She looked to Hamish.

'You'll do lass,' he said, his own tears not far off. He reached out for a comforting hand.

As she finished drying her eyes, Bella patted her back pocket, to touch the comforting presence of her mobile. She couldn't feel it, there was just empty denim. She sighed, she must have lost it, not that it mattered, nothing did anymore. It was probably still on the sofa, perhaps she had dropped it when learning the news of…she started crying again as she thought of her loss and how she was going to break it to her fiancé Irvine, Paul's best friend. His intended best man at their wedding. She tried to look in the mirror through her flow of tears, but she was too

hazy, just like she would be for a few months to come.

Feeling numb, like she was cast in a drama programme and

was acting out her role, she turned and unlocked the toilet

and walked back to her parents.

Chapter 9

'Whatever has gone on, you fix it, you hear me Joe, you fix it. I've lost one grandchild, I don't want you alienating my other,' declared Ruthie to her weeping husband.

'But Cameron, he should be allowed to go to the funeral, he was his nephew,' insisted Joe to his wife. He reached up to his shoulder for his tea towel.

'Put that bloody rag down and you pick up that phone and apologise to our son. Call yourself a father and grandfather. I heard you, and so did the girls. Bloody disgrace, wanting him to arrange the funeral. HOW BLOODY DARE YOU!' she vented.

Joe flinched. He dropped the tea towel as if he were a frightened matador dropping his cape at the sight of a raging bull. 'But...'

'No bloody buts either. I've bitten my tongue for years over what happened with Cameron. We should have gone to the police ourselves over what he did to that young lassie. I've never understood how you convinced her father to hush it all up. You pick up that phone and make things up with Hamish, he's enough to be coping with without carrying the sins of the father,' she pointed to the house telephone, its resting mouthpiece and earpiece speaking silent volumes.

Joe visibly recoiled from his wife. He'd never seen her so upset and so forthright. He wanted to pick up the tea towel, his comforter; but he knew better. He looked to the phone and carefully thought about what he would do. 'I'll go outside, have a smoke and then text him, he'll not be wanting me to call him whilst he is at the chapel of rest. A text message is less intrusive.' He scuttered off, leaving his wife to gently weep over the loss of her grandchild.

Bella walked over to her parents. A young couple were now in the seats opposite. She couldn't help but notice how red and sunken their eyes were. '*Oh, the poor man and woman must have lost a child too,*' she thought. But then she looked at their scabs and sores around their mouths, hands and neck. She glanced down their arms and noticed the dull purple-blue bruising from their wrists up along their forearms along with the faint tell-tale signs of scarlet track marks. She quickened her step and sat between the safety of her parents just as the young woman was self-consciously pulling down her stained sweater sleeves.

Hamish and Bella were about to take hold of her hand when the door to the side of them opened with a faint electronic buzz. A smartly dressed woman in a dark blue two-piece suit and black hosiery stepped through. As her heels clicked past the door it sprang back with a dull thud, shattering the solemn silence of the waiting area. She looked across to Hamish and a quick, mildly surprised look crossed her face. She walked over to him with her hand outstretched. 'Mr Dewart?' she enquired in a whispered conspiratorial voice.

'Aye.' Hamish replied, deliberately using a normal level of voice. He hated funereal voices with their hushed and self-pitying reverent tones. The dead and death was nothing to fear, nor seen as sacred. He had long ago shelved his belief in a God when he'd dealt with the truck incident in Belize. How could a loving, caring God take all those sons away from mothers in such a ghastly fashion? How could He do it to them?

'I'm Catriona, I'm your police liaison officer. We spoke briefly on the phone this morning,' she stated, unknowingly interrupting his reverie.

Hamish took the proffered hand, shook it and let it go. He used his now free hand to signal across to his wife and daughter. 'This is Bella, Paul's sister and my wife, Paul's mum.'

'Alison,' she interjected as she shook hands with Catriona.

Catriona continued in the hushed voice, 'I'm so sorry for your loss, and for the way Paul died.'

'Do you have the bastard, is he here?' demanded Hamish.

Alison put a hand on her husband's shoulder, not to restrain him, but to remind him that their daughter was here. The special communication between husband and wife was once more passed between them, without words.

'Please be assured Mr and Mrs Dewart,' Catriona looked between the two and then across to their daughter, 'and Bella, that the other driver is now in police custody. He will be interviewed later today.'

'You mean when the swine has sobered up?' interjected Hamish. He felt Alison's grip on him tighten. He took a deep breath in and relaxed his shoulders, trying to relieve his tension.

'I am aware that you know that the other driver was drunk. I can tell you that he failed a breathalyser test at the scene. After his injures were treated at the Foresterhill Hospital, he was taken here for a blood test, which we believe he will also fail. It can take several weeks to get the accurate results back, which the Procurator Fiscal office will use as part of their evidence to bring him to trial. We will do everything by the book and keep you abreast of information. You can also dial 101 at any time to seek information. I shall write down the crime number that you need to quote,' she reached into her pocket for a pen and opened up the clipboard that she had been carrying. Catriona then scrolled through a sheet of paper that she carefully hid from the family and scribbled away on a piece of paper that was tucked under the sleeve of the clipboard folder. She passed it to Hamish who simply took it and placed it in his pocket without reading it.

'Just make sure he goes to jail for this, he effectively murdered my son,' replied a resigned Hamish.

Quickly changing the subject, she said, 'I hadn't realised that you were bringing your family Mr Dewart. I understood from our phone call that it would just be you, only,' she unconsciously used the double-negative for emphasis. Catriona looked across to the young couple and crumpled her nose, as if in disgust. Remembering the situation, she looked back to the family and said in a soft voice, 'it's just that we've had a murder and I can only allow you to see Paul for the purposes of identification. You'll have plenty of time to see Paul at the undertakers, you see his PM is scheduled in thirty minutes and then he can be transferred to…' she stopped talking to allow Hamish or Alison to interject with the name of their preferred undertaker.

They didn't take the hint immediately. Hamish ruminated for a second, looked to the young couple, and said, 'Our son takes our priority, can we see him now please. We'll be using the local undertaker. We'll be going together, as a family.'

'Oh,' replied Catriona, hesitant for a second. She then quickly jotted something down on her piece of paper and closed the folding clipboard, hiding her furtive form. 'Okay, this way please. I'm afraid we must descend two flights of stairs.' She turned around and reached for her lanyard and security name badge, which she pressed to the lock mechanism. It gave a buzz like an angry bee whose feeding at the nectar had been disturbed. The family followed, Bella reached out and took her mother's hand whilst Hamish kept the door open for them. Alison gave her hand a squeeze and whispered, 'You're doing well Bella, be brave,' and they both followed the authoritative clicking of Catriona's heels.

His hand shook as he reached up for the butt of his cigarette. He grabbed it and flicked it, almost in disgust with it or himself, across to his neighbour's garden, a wry smile fleetingly crossed his face. *'That'll teach him to complain about the height of my hedging.'* He watched it settle on the grass, with the others that had been dampened down in the rains of last night. His smile had now faded, and he looked over his shoulder, through to the kitchen door and into the lounge, where his wife sat with her hands to her face. Her crying was making her shoulders convulse and pump more tears from her eyes. He did not feel proud, this was a low moment, even for him. He thought the lowest point of his life had been when he had told the father of the girl that he knew about his affair and would tell the wife about the young floozy in the fish factory. His silence had been bought, but at a price. Joe had been assaulted in Bridge Street, late one night after a work's do. His fractured ribs had taken weeks to heal and the pain from this and the kicks to his face had taken longer to stop hurting. Though he couldn't prove it, this being a time before CCTV was ubiquitous, he knew it was the girl's uncles. He grimaced at the recollection of the physical pain. But this loss of Paul was a right gut-wrenching loss, his only grandson. He knew Cameron would father no child, no respectable lassie went near him, his reputation went before him, like a dark ominous cloud of hate. He was proud of his family name, and proud of both sons, despite everything. He just wanted his family to be whole again. He little knew or could empathise with that this is what his younger son wished too.

Joe ceased his ruminations and reached into his pocket for his mobile phone. He pressed his forefinger to the on button and it magically read his fingerprint, a trick that Paul had taught him only the other week. 'It's for security grandad,' he'd said, 'in case your phone gets nicked. It's also quicker to turn on this way.'

'Oh, it's not right, not Paul,' he wailed as he tapped onto the green message's icon. It displayed the blue and grey typed conversation he had recently been exchanging with Cameron. He'd lost another job, rumours had followed him into his new workplace. He thought about letting him know about Paul, but he resisted that temptation. What good would that do? He'd tell him face to face. Not that his older son would be bothered, he'd had virtually no contact with Paul and Bella. Hamish had seen to that.

Family get-togethers at weddings and anniversaries had been strained. God knows what his sister's family thought of it all, though they must have known. Ruthie's side of the family knew. He could see it in their faces. Villages around here, and even the city, were hotbeds of gossip.

He clicked through and found Hamish's name. It was lower down the list because he seldom texted or even phoned his younger son. Someone had taken it upon themselves to write a letter to Hamish, years ago, laying out just what his brother had done, and how his father had intervened. It wasn't signed and there was no address. But the anonymous letter had been postmarked Aberdeen.

He hesitated as he thought about what he wanted to send and what he should send. He shrugged his shoulders and typed away.

They followed Catriona down the steps, taking their time, as if unconsciously delaying the inevitable and having to face reality. Uniformed police officers ran past them. Not off to a shout, but darting in and out of corridors and stairwells, on their way to the canteen or changing rooms, glad of the rest from their busy day. The family unit did not take them in, they were so caught up in grief.

Catriona stopped at the very bottom, turned to ensure the trio were still with her, and walked over to a door, that was ironically situated next to a lift. The quartet could have taken it to save them the rush of the officers around them. This too was lost on the family. Catriona waved her pass at the scanner and the door buzzed. She opened the door for the family and waved them through to a small corridor.

That's when the smell hit Alison and Hamish. That unmistakable smell of disinfectant, body fluids, death and misery. It hung in the air like a spectre at a haunting. The mortuary smell; they eyed one another knowingly.

There were several closed doors and in the corridor was a row of seats. These were more comfortable looking than the ones in reception. They were made of fabric and a deep mahogany wood and on a matching table between them was a box of tissues. Alison noted that the tissue box was empty. She knew what these rooms were used for and why the tissue box was empty. She wondered which room her son, her Paul, slept the eternal sleep. She gasped.

Hamish reached for her hand. 'You two sit down, I'll do this,' he ordered, once more in control and trying to be the dutiful husband and father.

Bella reached for both of their hands. 'No, we do this as a family,' she insisted.

Both parents accepted her hands and simultaneously gave them a squeeze.

'I'll take you in to see Paul in a moment. I'll need you to formally tell me that it is Paul, Mr Dewart. And I'll need you to sign a form before you go,' she resisted looking at her watch. There are seats in the room, could you please sit down when I go in. Please come out when you are ready. I'll open the curtain and then pop out to give you some privacy.'

'Curtain?' questioned Bella who was the only one not familiar with mortuaries and chapels of rest.

'Over the glass. There are two curtained areas and I will pull back the one that shows you Paul. He'll be resting on a trolley behind the glass. He does have some facial injuries, I must warn you of that,' heeded Catriona.

'I don't understand,' Bella questioned. She turned to her parents, 'Mum and dad, what does she mean.'

Her parents let go of her hands and stepped closer to her and embraced her whilst Catriona continued to explain.

'I'm so sorry. I thought you knew. You aren't allowed to be near Paul until after he is released into the care of your undertaker. Normally the police officers that broke the news of his death would have explained.'

Peeking out from their loving embrace, looking like a lost child, and feeling like one, Bella weakly asked, 'You mean I can't give my brother one last hug?'

'No lass,' answered her father. 'Not until they've finished their tests. There will be a court case over the accident. They have to treat Paul as evidence.'

'But he's not evidence dad, he's Paul, my brother,' wept Bella.

'I know lass, I know.' He stroked her hair and continued to embrace her, trying desperately to offer comfort from this grievous situation they had been flung into. He then thought of his actions in the early hours. 'But we'd only get in trouble ourselves if we try and get to Paul. We must let the professionals do their job and guide us in the correct actions that need to take place. There will be plenty of time to see Paul at the undertaker and you'll have Irvine with you as well as us.'

Catriona, inwardly sighed, acknowledging that Hamish would be of no further trouble to her, nor to her fellow police officers, after the events at the accident scene. 'I'll take you in now,' she prompted, trying desperately to get the balance of compassion and urgency. She wasn't looking forward to asking that young couple in reception to identify those three bodies. They'd soon be shooting-up to help them recover from identifying the mangled faces. Catriona herself would be needing a stiff drink at the Illicit Still pub this evening after seeing those three corpses. She quickly checked the room number against her clipboard and opened room three.

'How busy does it get here, that there are three viewing rooms?' wondered Hamish as he walked with his girls to be with his son, so that they could be a family again for one last time. He ushered Bella to the seat in the middle, so that he and Alison could comfort her. They sat down in the seats and stared ahead to the red velvety curtains in front of them. Another set of matching curtains was to the left of Alison and she turned her head in instinct to them. Whoever had arranged them had not closed them properly. Through a small gap she could see mousey-brown hair. It was set in a style that she'd combed for many years. Her shoulders drooped as she gave a small gasp which was unheard by her family over the voice of the police liaison officer, giving information that she did not take in, her world had just collapsed in turmoil. She felt dizzy and a head-rush of emotions threatened to overwhelm her as she fought to stay sat on her seat.

'I'll pull back the curtain and leave you to your thoughts and prayers, once again I'm so sorry for your loss,' said Catriona in that hushed tone that Hamish was beginning to really dislike.

Bella and Hamish looked ahead and were surprised when she leant over and pulled the cord to their left. The curtain opened with a swishing noise, as if it were a stage curtain about to reveal a macabre performance. Catriona then swiftly moved out of their way and discretely left the room.

Alison was on her feet, her left hand went to the glass, her palm caressed the pane, whilst her fingers were splayed out, as if trying to reach through to run her fingers through her son's hair. She had inadvertently carried Bella to the glass, she was still holding her hand and had forced her to her feet and to Paul's side. 'Oh, my poor boy!' Alison wailed.

Hamish was on his feet and enveloped his girls into a tight embrace, with them next to the glass and his towering bulk hunkered over them, as if trying to protect them from falling debris. Only he could not protect them from this peril, bereavement just ripped you apart and left wounds that would take months and even years to heal, if ever.

Alison let go of Bella's hand and she reached over and clung to her husband as she felt her legs go soft. It felt like some mischievous cricketer had whacked her behind her knees. Hamish supported her and kept a hand around his daughter.

'He looks just like he is asleep,' said Bella, 'I didn't know what to expect, but he looks so peaceful, except for the cuts and gashes. Would he have suffered dad?' She looked to her brother as her father pondered how to answer the heart-breaking question. She willed for the purple velvet covering to move, to rise in the air with a triumphant life-affirming movement. She wished that one of his hands were uncovered so that she could check it for colour and signs of life, for it to peel back the drape and shout 'gotcha,' and for this to be all one sick joke. But she knew it wasn't. Paul's cut, bruised and deeply-gashed face was testament to that.

'No lass,' lied her father for the first time to her, 'he wouldn't have felt a thing. He's at peace.'

Alison wept, tears flowing down her cheeks like a deluge of rain in a thunderstorm. A part of her had hoped that the police had it wrong, that Hamish mistook someone else in that field, but now reality had hit home, and she sobbed like only a mother could at losing the most precious thing in the world, her child. She took herself away from Hamish's embrace and Bella's tight grip on her hand and crouched over to the nearest chair and sat down, head in hands and wept.

Bella thumped the glass, 'It's not right dad, he shouldn't be lying there. That drunk took our Paul away from us.' She thumped the glass again, 'I need to give him a hug, to tell him that I love him, why can't we be next to him.'

Hamish looked about him, impotent to make this better. He cuddled his daughter, ran his hands through her hair and made 'shhing' noises. 'I know lass, but there is nothing we can do. The police have strict procedures and will not deviate from them. Let's try and remember Paul for all the fun we had together. You were a wonderful pair and filled our lives with joy. He knew that you loved him.'

Alison stood up and reached over for her daughter, clinging to her tightly, rocking her like she did as a colic-ridden infant, but no amount of gentle swaying would ease her daughter's pain. Nevertheless, she stood with her daughter for several minutes and held her tight with each fresh convulsion of tears that swept through her body like a tidal wave. She signalled the release of this grief-embrace by patting her on the back and ushered her to a seat. Her own tears were still flowing as she handed a nearby box of tissues to her daughter. She was relieved to see that these were full because her own supply in her pockets were all wet and used.

Hamish took the time to place both hands on the window, as if to reach out and hold his son, to pull him from his resting place and give him one last loving embrace. His hands circled the glass as if to replicate the movement he so yearned for, culminating in letting him back down to rest and then running his fingers down his cheek, as if acknowledging how handsome he was, despite the facial wounds so violently forced upon his innocent face. Then they suddenly dropped to his side, his shoulders drooped, and his forehead slumped to the glass with a dull thud which was not heard over the crying and wailing in the room. He was resigned to the inevitability of it all. Tears fell silently from his eyes, they were drowned out by the weeping from behind him.

'Well, have you done it?' questioned Ruthie as she made to reach for her walking stick.

'Almost, I'm just trying to find the right words,' sighed Joe as she walked further into the lounge, to the settee. Recognition as to what he'd done was beginning to settle hard upon his shoulders.

'Let me see then,' demanded his wife as she hobbled over to join him.

Joe sprang up, 'I'll do it in my own time, maybe give it an hour or so. They'll still be in the chapel of rest. He took his mobile phone back out of his pocket as he walked into the kitchen. He studied the screen, which read, 'Son, your

mother wants me to say that I'm so sorry for what I said.'
He considered it for a moment or two, his head going
inquisitively from side to side as he thought. He then
reached over with his other index finger and pressed the
delete button and watched sternly as his words were
deleted one by one until only a blankness was before him.
He then started typing.

She paced the corridor, deep in thought about the three
bodies that she would have to uncover for the next set of
relatives to identify. Her heels went clicking as fast as her
imagination at the horrors that would be beneath those
fresh sheets. She'd have to help take off the covers and
then replace them with the ever-present velvety drape in
that off-purple colour that she knew to only be used for
mortuary chapels of rest. The intricate embroidery around
the hems and the cross patterned onto the centre was often

overlooked by most families. Though they were etched in her mind, every single body and surviving family member came to her on her most troubled nights. The screams of the mothers were the worst. This drape was passed from body to body like a morbid game of pass the parcel. Only there were no winners in this macabre form of entertainment. Only losers in the ultimate game of chance, with the runners-up having to pick up the scattered pieces.

She stopped her pacing and turned to face room two, the larger of the viewing rooms. Set aside for bigger family groups to come and peer through the window, into a display that was as still as a shop's fashion parade revealing that year's trends and fashion on dummies twisted into human like form. Or, in the next case, for two bodies to be exhibited, side by side, for the same family corpses. In this case, it was brother and sister, killed by an estranged father. *'FUCK!'* she inwardly screamed. She started pacing again as her anxiety levels rose and pumped past the danger zone altitude.

'What makes a father do that to two young children, still in infant school and barely out of training pants and nappies,' she angrily thought. *'They had their whole life ahead of them and their bastard of a father shoots the life out of them whilst they sleep, to get back at his wife for walking out on them and taking a new lover.'* Both boyfriend and mother were now sat in reception and desperately needing a new fix. She hoped that a special place in Hell existed for such evil men. The cowards and vile bastards of society who snatched life from innocents through their selfish actions. Much like the fuckwit upstairs who was sobering up in a cell after taking Paul's life.

This thought snapped her out of her reverie and to the present cries coming from the room to her left. She could hear the banging on the purposely reinforced glass, specially crafted for these sad times. Not every family did this, though when they did it felt to her like they were knocking on the gates of whatever astral plain spirits went to. She often sat here and wondered what would happen if they got a reply. Would they ask to be with the newly departed spirit, or demand they return to their often disfigured or aged body? She stopped her frantic clicking on the floor, and her daft thoughts, and took her heels to the comfy seats and sat down with a deeply-felt sigh. '*I'll give it another month, and if I don't feel any better about the job, then I'll request a transfer back to being normal plod. I know where I am there, catching thieves, convincing women to testify against their raised fists partners, heck, even giving directions at road traffic collisions would be better than this.*' She looked to her watch and wondered if she'd have time to pee between viewings.

'I think that we may have to leave Paul and free up Catriona's time for the other family,' said Alison, now composed. She went over to the glass and mouthed 'I love you,' through the pane and placed her hand on it for one final time. She then went over to her daughter, hunched down beside her and placed her hand on her knee. 'Come and say goodbye to Paul sweetie.' She reached up and took Bella's hand and they stood up in unison. They walked over to the window, leaving Hamish on his seat gathering his thoughts. After a few moments he stood up and walked forward, gathered his daughter and wife around his arms and said, 'Goodbye Paul, you were a lovely son and brother. We love you. We'll see you at the undertakers.' He then, reluctantly, guided his family out of the door, ignoring the unopened curtain. If there was another body behind that one, he did not care. He had seen enough death to last him a lifetime. And the one body that he wanted to hold, to wash and dress for its final journey, he could not.

Chapter 10

He sat in the car, slumped in the driver's seat and toyed with the coin-like token, like a poker player wondering which move to make with the card's that life had dealt him. He was numb with the inevitability of it all. He wanted to grab the steering-wheel and wrench it from its holding, he did not want life directing him in this direction. He wanted to grab the gearstick and reverse back time.

'We are ready when you are Hamish. I don't want to be here any longer. Paul's gone, and we need to go home and start phoning round our family and friends. He's with my mum and dad now, they will take care of him now until we are reunited one day.'

Hamish sighed, as he turned on the ignition. He wished that he could have faith like Alison, he often wondered how she had such blind belief in a higher being after all the things she'd seen as a nurse, especially on the oncology unit. How could a loving God form such cancerous tissues and cause such life-ending diseases. Though Alison didn't attend church regularly, he knew that she often prayed and read parts of her bible. He put the car into gear and as he reversed, he caught his daughter's eye and tried to smile warmly to her so that she didn't feel lonely in the back seat. He failed miserably, she was alone now, she'd lost her brother and best friend.   There would always be a spare, empty seat wherever they went. In the car, at restaurants and even the cinema. Each of them would be looking at it and wishing that Paul could once more occupy it. He drove to the barrier, wound down the window and pushed the token into the waiting machine. The security barrier slowly rose up, as if a soldier giving a graveside salute to a fallen comrade. It lingered in the air, awaiting a command from its senior officer, the sensor that would relay the order to lower, when the family passed on from this fateful place. Hamish drove on and turned out of the police headquarters and on through the road by Marischal Square, its elegant new building lost on him. He would not be in the frame of mind to admire the Leopard statue today. He then allowed the car to sit at the crossroads, engine idling, like his mind, it ticked over, awaiting fresh instructions. His hand wrapped around and grasped the gearstick, as tight as he'd have hugged his son, if only the police would have allowed it.

Alison reached over and placed her hand on his. He relaxed a bit at her warmth. She rubbed her fingers lovingly around his and he could feel her wanting him to push his hand forward, ever so gently. 'Put her in first gear and then turn left and then left again,' she whispered encouragingly.

Now he knew why she hadn't sat in the back with Bella.

His need for her support was greater. She knew, like she

always seemed to know, that he'd be tired after the night

they'd had and that this whirlwind of emotions would

eventually plunge, be calmed, and cause an adrenaline

slump. As if to reinforce this thought he let out an

involuntary yawn as he obeyed her commands and

navigation, and drove slowly away from the Council

buildings at Marischal College, the brickwork lovely and

shiny when compared to the church next door that had not

been deep-cleaned of decades of soot. The Council never

spent a penny more than it needed to, not even for God.

Alison interrupted his thoughts again and said, 'turn

another left and then go in the right lane and turn right.'

Hamish obeyed, glad of someone to tell him what to do,

'*a bit like being back in the army*,' he thought. He'd

missed the structure of the military when he first came out, but soon found similar regimentation in the NHS.

'Okay, now turn into Morrison's, I think we all need a cup of coffee, especially you, before we have the long drive home,' ordered Alison.

Hamish agreed and pushed up his indicator and drove on through the green light, just as his phone gave two beeps. He had a text message awaiting him in his jacket pocket.

She held the handle at forty-five degrees and began her incision with a decisive thrust. It's razor sharp blade penetrated deep and sliced through the flesh and exposed the inners as she cut deeper. Her eyes pricked at the thought of what she was doing, had to do as her duty. Tears sprang to her eyes, blurring her vision, causing her focus to waver from the task in hand. She cut deeper and heard the satisfying pop that told her that she had reached her target. She reached down and grasped and separated the flesh, fingers coiling expertly around the outer flesh, gathering it up and laying it aside. She returned to the inner of the onion and grasped her knife once more and began to finely chop the vegetable, before adding it to the pot. '*They'd need something warm and filling when they return*,' she thought, '*and this was their favourite whenever she made it for her Bill, and they came for tea.*' She sighed as she thought of the pain they would be in and remembered her loss. It never leaves you, though it gets easier to live with, to build a life around. Though no amount of padding really detracts from the pain. '*This was the least she could do*,' thought Molly as she reached for the carrots.

Alison took the cup from the coffee machine after the whirring, frothing, cycle had finished. She placed it on the tray alongside that of her husband's and Bella's apple juice. She pointed at the array of sandwiches, biscuits, cakes and crisps. 'Would you like something to eat love?'

'I don't think I can eat mum, I'm sorry. I know that I am hungry, but I just can't face it,' replied Bella.

Her father nodded, 'Me neither.' He pushed the tray along towards the till. 'You two go and sit down and I'll join you in a moment,' he fished about in his jacket and realised he'd left without his wallet.

Alison pushed a tenner into his hand.

Hamish smiled grimly, 'I'm glad one of us is thinking straight today.'

She smiled back, 'You are doing just fine love, we'll grab that table over there,' she pointed, 'It'll be quieter.'

Hamish nodded and watched them go, his heart went out to them both.

Joe looked at his mobile phone and then pocketed it with a shrug. He'd had to let his son know how he felt. The text was sent, and that was that. He reached into his other pocket and took out a cigarette packet and with deft fingers tapped a cigarette out and lit it with the small lighter he always kept in the box, a thoughtful present from Cameron. He took a long drag and exhaled smoothly, before breaking into a coughing fit. He then gathered up the phlegm and spat out, towards his prick of a neighbour. It fell short and landed on his own patio, like a splattered gift from a passing seagull. He stood up straight and walked down his back steps, towards his greenhouse and his prized fuchsias, stored away from the winter frosts, ready to be planted out in the spring. He slid open the door and entered the warmth of his greenhouse, thanks to his old trusty paraffin heater. The first fuchsia was appropriately called 'Army Nurse.' He loved the vibrant reds of this plant, a gift from Paul, who had bought two.

One for his veteran dad and one for his grandfather. Joe

picked it up and caressed its pot, as if cradling an urn of

ashes. He absently wondered if Paul would be cremated or

buried. He hoped that it was a closed casket funeral. He

didn't have as strong a stomach as Hamish, and Paul

would have been in a right mess after the accident. He

didn't envy his son viewing him, but then he was probably

used to such sights.

Hamish shrugged out of his jacket and draped it over the

back of his chair. He sat down and reached over for his

coffee and cupped it with both hands. He drew physical

comfort from its warmth and in juxtaposition to this action,

he started to blow on the liquid to cool it down.

'I think you had a text dad, while you were driving,'

informed Bella as she wondered if she should ask him if

she could have a loan of his mobile phone in order to ring Irvine, she so wanted to hear his reassuring voice.

As if reading her thoughts, Alison interjected by saying, 'God, what do we say to everyone. They are all going to be so upset when we tell them that Paul has died,' she burst into fresh tears.

Hamish put down his coffee and reached across the table and grasped his wife's hands. 'Let me do that love. Let's just sit quietly and drink and think of Paul. Leave me to ring around when we get home. Molly may well have rung some folk already, like your fellow Elders at the Kirk. This is a time for their fellowship and for your Minister to give you comfort. If I know Molly, she'll have a huge pan of broth on the go as we speak, and a mountain of sandwiches.'

Alison smiled weakly, 'Like I did for her when Bill passed, bless her.'

'Aye, you Scots lassies and your need to feed us lads up,' he looked sadly at the empty seat. '*Why were café and restaurant tables always set up for four. Our standard family group has been cut at the core,*' he thought grimly. He reached behind him for his mobile and placed it on the table whilst he fished in his other pocket for his reading glasses.

Alison and Bella took half-hearted sips of their drinks, oblivious to the other diners who noisily went about their lunch hour with much haste. Neither had the appetite to know that it was already early in the afternoon and that Hamish had been up for almost twelve hours and that Alison was also equally tired, despite her drug-induced sleep after the policemen left. Neither were watching the growing disbelief that Hamish was showing on his reddening face as it quickened to anger. 'I don't believe it. Now I know that he's never loved me as much as golden-boy Cameron. Today of all days,' said Hamish in a raised voice.

'What is it love, is it your dad?' asked Alison urgently as she reached for his mobile.

Hamish pushed it towards her, as if he wanted nothing more to do with the object on the table, the deliverer of bad news. 'He's no dad. A father would smother his son with love on a day like today, not be more concerned about the family paedo.'

'Wait, what!' exclaimed Bella in bewilderment.

Hamish looked around him, remembering where he was and lowered his voice. 'Sorry lass. I know it's not the place, but it's time for us to have that chat I promised you earlier. I would have had it then, but you were so upset, and we had to be at the police station as soon as we could.' He took off his reading glasses, folded them and pointed to his mobile that Alison was now staring at in shock and

166

disbelief. 'It's probably best if you begin by reading the text to Bella.'

'He's so well out of order. We haven't even booked an undertaker yet,' said Alison, her eyes fixed firmly to the screen.

'What does it say,' asked Bella, more urgency in her voice. 'Who's it from?'

Alison groaned as she slid the phone to her husband. She knew that this would cut to Hamish's heart. He reached over and took it from her and then powered it off, as if erasing the message from his mind.

'It's from my dad,' sighed Hamish. 'It said that you cannot ban Cameron from the house of God, it is a public place. He means that we cannot stop Paul's uncle from attending his funeral.'

'But why would he want to attend?' said a puzzled Bella. 'He didn't have anything to do with us. We didn't see him often. But when we did, he was always on the other side of the room at the few weddings and parties we went to.'

'It was us that kept him from you and Paul love. Your father and me. You see Cameron was a… ' Alison struggled to vocalise the right words. She turned to her husband for help.

'I don't know how to cushion the blow of this one Bella, so I'm just going to tell you straight out, no messing. Your uncle, my older brother, he interfered with a young girl. He was babysitting a neighbour's child. She was only nine years old and he made her, well he made her perform a sexual act, and not for the first time. The girl confided in a friend, she wanted to know if this was something all babysitters did, if it was normal. The friend then told her mum, who then told her husband and before you know it there was a lynch mob outside our house. I was only fourteen and got caught up in the backlash too. Dad seemed to be able to sort out the girl's family. I don't know how. He then sent Cameron on the trawlers, up MacDuff way, to get away from the gossip. But it followed him and years later, a bunk-mate found some distasteful material amongst Cameron's things, a magazine had fallen out during rough seas, so the rumours I've heard is that he's still, well, into young girls I guess you could say. My friends stopped speaking to me too and I didn't want to be in the area after that. Then a few weeks later dad was in the hospital for a night. When he came home, he was so bruised and battered, I could tell that he had been in a fight or set upon most likely.'

'I, I don't know what to say dad,' mumbled Bella, this new drama in her life was confusing her mind. She looked around her, worried that the other café users may have overheard. The groups of women were too deep in their own office gossip to give them any heed. 'Is that why you joined the army, you know, to get away?'

'Aye lass, I couldn't wait to leave home and put it all behind me and get away from my scheming dad and my paedo of a brother. But the upshot of it was that I was posted to the military hospital in Woolwich, where I met your mother and then you two came along soon after. I was more than happy.' He reached across and patted his daughter's hand, 'And proud of you both.'

'So, you see,' said Alison, reaching across to join the hand-holding, 'your dad and I were just trying to protect you from abuse, that's why we never left you alone with your uncle and why we weren't too bothered about your grandparents, on your dad's side, babysitting you. We never knew if they would take you to see Cameron, when he visited them on the boats, or would leave you with him alone, when he was on shore leave.'

'Oh, I didn't realise, I don't know what to say,' replied Bella as she bit her lip to stop herself crying once more, not just over these fresh revelations, but from all the emotions over the last few hours.

'I blame my dad,' stated Hamish as he withdrew his hand, sat back and looked down at his coffee. He took a reluctant sip, he had no appetite for anything. He looked out of the window to where two seagulls were fighting over a dropped sandwich. *'Probably discarded by a schoolkid when he found that the canteen lady had the audacity to add something healthy, like lettuce,'* he thought.

Alison looked across to him, 'For the abuse you mean?'

'Aye,' stated Hamish simply, reluctantly drawn back to his dark chain of thought, all ponderings over the bird life forgotten. He looked around him, as if seeking a new conversation with the gossiping office workers or the single folk staring at their phones and tablets.

'Why?' questioned Bella.

'Not just for the cover-up, but for the way he treats women. I've seen it with my mum, he really doesn't seem to care, doesn't have the emotional wherewithal. He's no empathy.' He looked to his wife and then his daughter as if weighing up what to say next. 'Och well, look, there's something I have to tell you,' he looked back to Alison. 'I didn't tell you everything about my childhood. I guess I was ashamed, and I saw how happy your childhood had been, I'd seen how loving your parents were to you and then how welcoming they were to me when we were dating. They were so over the moon when we got married and absolutely elated when we had the children. I saw into a normal family.'

'They loved you both,' interrupted Alison, looking to her daughter. 'They loved looking after you when we were both at work. Even when mum was dying, all they talked about was you and Paul. They looked forward to seeing you both, dressed in your smart primary school uniform, visiting the hospice when mum went into respite to give me a break.' She burst into fresh tears as she thought of her loss, and not just Paul. 'Dad died of a broken heart, and I think I will too.'

'That's why I don't want to tell you any more upsets love, let's just leave it for another time,' insisted Hamish as he held his wife's hand.

'No, I'm alright love, you continue,' replied Alison as she wiped her tears and blew her nose.

'Aye, well, remember I was just a young lad. It was a confusing time for me, I'd hit puberty, had trouble making friends at school. You see I was never allowed pals to come home, to play in my room, mum and dad didn't like it. I don't know why. But friends got fed up with me always being at their house and never being invited back to mine. Soon they stopped answering their door, I never got invited to parties and then, at school, they wouldn't talk to me, they'd huddle in groups and point at me, like they were gossiping. I learnt, years later, that my brother's reputation went before me. It turned out that he'd tried other things with other girls at the school. He was four years older than me, but the rumours persisted and folk thought, brother like brother.'

'Oh, that's sad dad,' said Bella reaching forward to clasp her dad's hands around his coffee cup. 'But why do you blame grandad?'

Hamish looked down at his coffee cup, mulling over what to say next. 'I hate secrets and lies,' he stated, thinking back to the lie he'd told his daughter about Paul not suffering. 'They destroy families, and I want us to stay together,' he looked up and glanced at his wife and daughter and then returned his hunched vigil over his coffee cup.

'Please tell us Hamish, no secrets please,' pleaded his desperate wife.

'Okay, though it's not so much a secret, as something that came out in therapy, years ago, when I saw the NHS psychologist, when work was hectic and events from the past overwhelmed me. She made me remember things that I'd buried and forgotten about from my childhood. It kind of explained why Cameron turned out the way he did. My saving grace was that I took myself off to my nana's.' He smiled briefly at the thought of his long-dead grandmother. He looked up to see his wife smiling at the memory of her too.

'She made me feel so welcome. She even turned off Coronation Street when she met me,' recalled Alison fondly.

Bella turned to her mother, puzzled.

'It was her favourite soap, in a time when video recorders were expensive and bulky. She had no way of recording the episode. There was no Netflix or catch up then, not even repeats.'

Bella's thoughts went to her phone and she wished that she could speak to Irvine now, she wanted to be the one to break the news of Paul's death. 'Oh,' she merely said.

'Yes, you see? It showed that she thought a lot of me.'

'That's more than my parents did. The psychologist told me over and over that I was neglected, abused emotionally. It took me a while to acknowledge that. When I did, I wasn't too sure that I wanted to leave you and Paul in their care, not that it was a problem because they never offered and always seemed to be too busy on the few, desperate occasions that we asked. But you had your uncles and aunties from your mum's side.' Hamish stopped to take a sip of his coffee and then said, 'They are going to be devasted.'

'We all are love,' replied Alison.

'That's why I can't understand dad's reaction. Why his first words were to ask if Cameron could arrange and come to Paul's funeral.'

'It's face love, they want the rest of the family, and their friends, to see what a lovely family you all are. If your brother is not there, and he won't be, I'll see to that, folks will ask you why not,' stated a defiant Alison.

'Oh loves, that's not all,' said Hamish looking down at his tepid coffee.

'I've always known there would be more Hamish. Remember, I saw how upset you were after each session, and how tired.'

'Dad worked in the oil rigs, those roughnecks earned their names. It was tough work, but they were worse than squaddies, vulgar and loud. Offshore, they could get all sorts and dad would come home with the vilest pornographic videos. Because he earned so much, we could afford a video recorder. A big thing it was, with a cable that ran across the room to operate the remote control. Shame he didn't think to buy nana one. She'd have loved to have been able to record things like Dallas when Des O'Connor was on the other channel.'

'Des who?' enquired Bella.

'Shh, let your dad go on,' berated Alison, though in a soft voice. She reached over and rubbed her husband's hands in encouragement.

'I don't know why, and even the psychologist couldn't explain it, but mum and dad would watch them in front of me and Cameron. This was a year or two before the babysitting incident. They were so vile. I'd be sat reading a comic in the lounge, I'd have been about twelve, the Eagle had just been revived. I loved Dan Dare. Then in would come mum and dad and then the TV went on and the video tape would go in the machine and then there were all sorts of groans and moans. This always attracted Cameron and the three would be glued to the screen. I always left and walked up to nanas. It just confused my young mind. I never understood mum's reactions of going along with it. She neglected to wash my clothes, and I didn't know how to use the machine. So, I started to smell of urine when I ran out of pants and trousers. That's really when I lost what few friends I had. I started to smell bad in class. I fell over and tore my trousers. I went around with a huge hole in my knee for weeks. That lasted a few months and soon nana was doing my laundry and letting me shower at her house. I often stayed for several nights a week. That's when I got my love for Dallas and musicals. She loved those.' Hamish sighed at the fond memory of his beloved grandmother which was in sharp contrast to the bad memories of his parents.

'Dad lost his job soon after, then had to work ashore. The videos stopped appearing and things settled down. But he was never a close father, he didn't take an interest in me. His own dad died at a young age, so I don't think he knew how to bring up two boys. I think, in his own way, that perhaps he thought that he was giving us sex education, though the videos are not how normal folk make love. I'm sorry. But looking back I think that's when Cameron got confused too. He would have been about fifteen or sixteen, in his last year at school and I think that's when he would have started his inappropriate behaviour. I often wonder if dad had never brought those pornographic videos home, then perhaps Cameron wouldn't have sexually assaulted the young girl. I'm so sorry,' he looked down at his coffee and swirled the cup to remove the creamy scum that formed around the inside.

'It's not your fault Hamish, I'm glad that you have told us. No more secrets. You've nothing to be sorry for. I think you are right. Cameron's mind would have been confused and warped. But it doesn't excuse what he did,' she said angrily, causing the café assistant who was busy clearing tables to look up sharply.

Oblivious to her stare, Hamish carried on, 'I couldn't tell nana what was going on, she and my grandad would have been angry with their daughter for watching such filth. She'd have been disgusted and I felt like it was a dirty secret, I felt so ashamed. I still feel guilt over what happened to that young lassie and perhaps others.'

Bella reached over and held her father's hands, 'I love you dad. Thank you for looking out for me and Paul. We always felt safe with you and our childhood was happy and fun.'

Hamish looked up, tears formed in his eyes as he patted his daughter's hands, not trusting his voice to reply to her.

Chapter 11

Isaac walked along the street, he was seldom seen outside his shop at this time of the day, he needed to work during the busy lunch hour when folk bought sandwiches and pies, freshly delivered by the local baker that morning. However, Sarah had insisted that she could manage without him for a little while. As he drew alongside the empty driveway he hesitated and rested his heavy load on the adjoining wall. He knew that Molly was the neighbour to this side, because his paper boys and girls used to deliver the evening paper to her Bill. It was soon cancelled after his death though, she much preferred seeing Jackie Bird on the telly in the evening and hearing it straight from her lips. Not that he had any youngsters delivering the paper now, Facebook and the other social media channels had dwindled down readership so much that it was no longer profitable to pay pocket money rates for delivery. He popped them through letter boxes to the few elderly people who had the time to read the printed word, but who felt too old to trust those new-fangled tablets and phones. The exercise around the village did him good, he enjoyed getting a bit of fresh air. He pondered over ringing the doorbell, but not seeing any cars, he realised that no-one was probably in.

He continued walking a few more paces and opened Molly's gates. She had no need for a car and preferred to save money and make use of her free bus pass. A local builder had built her a lovely pink granite wall and hung a new gate to keep in the terrier dog that she sometimes looked after for her friend. As he walked down the path, with the comfort box that they always gave to the recently bereaved, he was relieved to see Molly open the door. She wore a half-smile.

'I knew that this would have been far too heavy for you Molly, so I took the precaution of bringing it over.'

'Oh, that's so good of you Isaac, what a caring couple you and Sarah are. Would you be after taking it next door for me please, it does look over-heavy for me?' she asked whilst not waiting for a reply. 'You pop over and I'll follow with a key.' She grabbed a keyring from the hook on the wall and slipped effortlessly out of her slippers and into some slip-on shoes inside her porch, she then closed her own door and followed Isaac up her path.

Hamish's head nodded up and down as he struggled to fight his fatigue. He felt a hand rest on the steering wheel as he came to with a start, *'Christ! That's all we need, for me to crash into someone on today of all days.'* He quickly looked over to Alison who was giving him a knowing look. 'Sorry lass, it's been a long day,' he said meekly.

'I think that you should rest while I phone around my family and our friends. Take a wee nap when we get home.'

'I don't think I can Alison love,' though he knew he nearly did, just then, as the car had wandered over to the middle of the road. Fortunately, it was the post-lunch quiet time on the recently built dual-carriageway of the A90.

'Maybe not. But rest your eyes all the same. My pals and family would rather hear it from me. Your chums can wait until this evening, when they are home from work.'

'But the undertaker...'insisted Hamish.

'Can wait too Hamish, Paul won't go anywhere until they have finished their tests, which I don't think will be today. Besides, the police liaison woman knows we are using the local undertaker, she'll have all his details.'

'No, of course you are right.' He looked in the rear-view mirror, Bella had fallen asleep, despite, or because of the day's events. 'I'll drop off Bella at Irvine's first. I don't want her having to get the bus.'

'We'll drop her off on the way. She wants to see him alone, to break the news, then they'll need some time together. That's when you can have a nap, to prepare yourself for all the visitors. Irvine can drive her home, when she's ready.'

Isaac walked through to the kitchen with his box, he always found it a privilege to come into the recently bereaved family home to deliver the necessary food, drink and tissues. Things that folk would run out of given the Scottish tradition of going straight to the bereaved home to pay respects before the funeral was even booked. He placed it reverently on the kitchen table and looked up at the laminated paintings that adorned the wall. So obviously done by Paul and Bella as toddlers, and so lovingly preserved and cherished by their mother.

He patted the box, 'I guess I don't need to let you know what Sarah has packed,' stated Isaac, remembering the time that he had delivered just such a box to her on the day they'd learnt the sad news.

'No, and I so appreciated it. I'd nothing in the cupboards to offer guests, it was the last thing on my mind at the time.' She reached up and patted him on the shoulders. She knew that most, like hers, had been carefully selected and packaged by him. She'd wished he'd have taken payment then and knew that she shouldn't offer payment now. It would be refused. Sarah and he had received her grateful custom even more since then and the village had taken them to their hearts since this tradition started, even the most mean-spirited widower had his begrudged respect over their kindness. The old man down the road, who spent his retirement washing and polishing his car every day, like an idolised God, though he seldom drove for he had no friends to visit. Even he would go out of his way to say a few words whenever he saw Isaac.

Irvine came rushing out of the house as he saw the familiar car pull up to the kerbside. He bounded over to the vehicle and opened the passenger door with haste. Bella scrambled out and into his arms and burst into tears, real deep sobs of grief. He cradled her and held on tight, not knowing what to do or what to say. They stood there for a few minutes, coupled in their grief, as their tears flowed as one down each other's shoulders.

Alison and Hamish held each other's hands, the gear-stick acting as a barrier between the couple. They gave their daughter and her fiancé a respectful few moments. They were now learning to share the grief, to allow others to mourn for Paul. Each were wondering how Irvine seemed to know the sad news. After what seemed an age, Hamish stepped out and walked the few feet to them.

'You've heard then s...' He fell short of calling Irvine son, though he'd got in the habit of saying this over the years, his way of welcoming Irvine into the family fold. He could not bear to say it today. He was not sure if he would ever say it again.

The young couple broke off their embrace, though Bella slipped her hands around Irvine's waist for support. 'The newspaper, they had a photo on their Facebook page. I had hoped that he'd just be injured, but when I saw how upset Bella was, well...' he left his sentence unfinished as fresh tears fell and he turned and dropped into Bella's shoulder. Their tears fell once more, cascades of anguish gushing like a waterfall, though this was no scene of serene beauty.

Their gate sprang open again and they were joined by Irvine's dad who stretched out his hand to Hamish. Both dads took each other by the hand which developed into an awkward embrace, shoulders bumping inelegantly, like a half-hearted wrestling move gone wrong. 'I'm so sorry Hamish, is it true? It could only have been Paul's car.'

'Aye,' replied Hamish as he allowed Lenny to break off the embrace and pat him on the hand. He released himself from this grip, much to the relief of Lenny.

'Oh shit, oh man, I'm right sorry. He was a great boy,' he turned to look to the youngsters who were trying to console each other. 'I'll look after them both, don't you worry. I'll fetch her home in a few hours. Irvine couldn't reach her on the phone,' he awkwardly stated, though it was really a question.

'We've been at the police station, seeing Paul.'

'Ah,' replied Lenny, giving Hamish a pat on the shoulder, trying to reach out with some empathy. 'That can't have been easy, how's Alison bearing up?'

'She's stunned, we all are. We are still trying to make sense of it all. Bella hasn't eaten anything all day. Could you please make sure that she has something to eat? Sorry to ask.'

'Of course, dear chap, of course,' he nodded towards his house. 'Tricia has some sandwiches prepared, she's still in the kitchen. Shall I get her? No, sorry, I'm no good at all this, come inside, have you and Alison eaten?'

'No, we just can't face food now. We've had a cup of coffee. That'll do us. Alison is keen to phone her sisters and brother and I think that Bella just wants to be alone with Irvine.'

'Of course, of course,' replied Lenny as he turned to talk to his son. He wasn't there. He and Bella had taken themselves off, oblivious to all else in their shared grief. They were already climbing the stairs to the sanctuary of Irvine's bedroom.

It was now Tricia's turn to briskly walk down the path. Though she ignored the two men and went straight to the front passenger door, opened it, stooped down, and took Alison in her arms. 'Oh lass, it's so wrong. I'm so sorry to hear about Paul. Oh Bella, bless her, it's just such an awful thing to have happened.' She tried to rock her friend from side to side, but she still had her seatbelt on. 'Come away in and have a cup of tea.'

Alison, all cried out for the moment, said 'I wish we could, but I have to ring my family and tell them, so that they can arrange time off work for the funeral. We hope to have Paul to the undertaker tomorrow. Will you look after Bella please?' asked Alison, not really wanting to let go of her daughter, though knowing she was in safe hands.

'Of course, you don't have to ask. She and Paul are part of the family. Oh, the poor boy, so young.' She hugged Alison a bit closer. 'We'd hoped that it wasn't true, but it is, oh it's just so sad, you poor thing. It's not right.' She broke off her hug for her back was starting to hurt. 'Please phone us if there is anything we can do,' said Tricia as she straightened up.

Alison merely nodded, '*What could anyone do?*' she thought as she held back her tears.

Molly held back her net curtain as she watched Hamish reverse into his driveway. She resisted the urge to rush to them, to be with them in their grief. She knew, from her own experience, just how tired they would be. She had left notes around the kitchen. Instructions for heating the soup and how Isaac had kindly delivered some groceries, most of which were put away in cupboards and the fridge. She wasn't sure how long a respectful length of time would be; but thought perhaps thirty minutes would suffice. Enough time for them to have a cup of tea and take stock of that day's events.

Hamish locked the car and stared up at his house, their home for over a decade, the longest they'd ever been in a house. They'd moved a lot in the army and had settled here because Hamish had missed his native Scotland. They had wanted to put down roots and this village seemed as good a place as any. They'd been able to buy the house outright, thanks to their careful saving over the years. The children had finally been able to have a place to call home. Now their peaceful idyll had been shattered and Hamish wondered grimly if they would ever be happy again.

'Come away in Hamish,' said Alison, breaking his reverie. 'I'll make us a sandwich, and then I think you should nap whilst I phone my family. That'll take me a good hour, so I don't expect to see you for at least two hours.'

Hamish knew when not to argue and followed her inside. He hadn't the heart to wave to Molly.

Irvine cradled Bella's face and whispered, 'I love you,' as fresh tears fell from her face. He felt so powerless as he watched his love weep. She nodded in return, unable to even whisper back. They fell into each other's arms again, Irvine not realising that this is exactly what Bella needed for he'd had no experience of death before. He had no insight into an unexpectedly shattered life. If his parents had been able to see them, instead of pacing nervously downstairs, then they would have been proud of him.

Alison ladled the heated broth into two small bowls. She ignored the fresh bread rolls for she knew that neither she, nor her husband, would feel like eating them. She knew that it would be a struggle for them both to sup at the soup. Without a word, she walked over to their dining table and placed a bowl in front of Hamish, who had been sat staring at the wall whilst the broth had simmered away in the huge pot and Alison had read Molly's instructions. She placed her own bowl down and then handed her husband a spoon. 'Here love, we must eat, we have to keep strong. For Bella and each other. Then you must rest.'

He took the spoon and a brief smile passed his lips. 'I know lass, I know, though I don't rightly feel like it, even though Molly knows fine well that it is my favourite, our favourite. Her special recipe too.'

Alison held up her spoon for him to see, then, once she was satisfied that his gaze was now focused, she used her spoon to ladle up some of the broth. She nodded to her husband and watched as he copied her act, and spoon for spoon, they slowly refuelled.

Tricia knocked lightly on the bedroom door, a tentative tap, like a nervous candidate entering a room for a job interview. After a few moments she coyly stepped into her son's bedroom, a room she rarely entered since he reached adulthood and was finished being taught to make his own bed and iron his own clothes. She did not want her fate, a domestic goddess, to fall upon the young shoulders of Bella. Nor did she want for this bereaved fate to fall upon her. 'Oh lass, I'm so sorry to hear about your brother,' she said as she deliberately sat between the couple. She reached out and embraced her soon to be daughter-in-law. 'You come down when you are ready, I've promised your mum that I'll make you something to eat. I've made your favourite sandwich and there is fresh orange juice on the table.' She patted Bella's shoulder and broke off the embrace, turned and gave her son a quick cuddle, as if to say, 'You are doing the right thing,' and then rose and left the room, closing the door gently behind her.

There was a timid tap on the back door and then a key fumbled in the lock and Molly entered their family home. 'I hope you don't mind me coming in, I thought I'd see how you both are. Have you had a nice cup of tea and something to eat?'

Hamish smiled affectionately. 'I do love your broth Molly. It was just what we both needed. It's warmed me back up. I've felt so cold, right down to my bones. I can't seem to get warm since...' A momentarily sadness passed through him as he thought how cold Paul would be in the mortuary, he'd probably be put back in one of the fridges with just a simple sheet to cover him. He really did hate the cold.

Molly saw this wretched look pass over him and put her hand on his shoulder. He clasped it, as if to seek warmth and strength from it, and then it was carried off as he rose to his feet so that he could rinse out his bowl. 'You leave that to me, you just sit down, and I'll make you a cup of tea,' she insisted, taking the empty bowl from him. She could hear a one-sided conversation from through the lounge. 'I'll close this kitchen door, that'll be Alison phoning relatives then?' She remembered how difficult this was after her Bill passed away. 'She'll not be wanting to hear me clatter about. How was the police station? Och,' she replied to her own question without giving Hamish a chance to answer, 'that's a stupid question, if ever there was one.' She closed the door quietly and then walked over to the sink to rinse off the bowl and spoon.

Hamish laughed, despite the circumstances. 'It's fine Molly, though it was awful. I can't take my girls' pain away. I can't bring our Paul back.' He looked solemn once more.

'No, and nor should you. They both need to cry and grieve for your son, her brother. Their pain is their bodies telling them that they loved so hard and so much. They wouldn't be human if they didn't. Take that man around the corner, the one who lost his wife three years ago. He went straight out to his shed and carried on hammering away the second her body was taken away by the undertakers. Even on the morning of her funeral he was banging away, working to complete orders, so full of his own importance. He's not grieved at all. He's either in denial or he didn't love her. Mind you, he used to belt her something awful, poor lass. I doubt he loved her or misses her. So, you let the girls cry for all they are worth, and you do the same, because everybody knows how much Paul was loved and will be missed.'

Bella toyed with her chicken, bacon and lettuce sandwich, taking hamster-like bites from it to appease Tricia. She was sat in Irvine's lounge, and for once the television was not blaring out the rolling news that the couple liked to follow. Irvine sat next to her, at the small table, playing around tentatively with his lunch too. Lenny was jumping up and down from his chair, his nervous energy needing to be expunged.

Tricia, knowing this, told him, 'Away to the shop and get some milk Len, the blue topped one,' she helpfully suggested, knowing that he'd only get there and phone her to ask.

'Right you are,' he said as he sprang once more from his armchair, grateful for something to do. He left the room, stopping briefly to place his hand on Bella's shoulder.

'You'll have to get used to our Len and his funny ways one day Bella. He's not used to interacting with folk much. It comes with working from home in his den,' she nodded to the back of their garden.

Bella nodded, smiled briefly and took another bite of her sandwich to appease Tricia. '*Was it wrong to be enjoying her favourite snack, the Scooby snack, that Lenny called it, whenever he came in for his lunch, when poor Paul was probably being cut up and dissected as she ate?*' wondered Bella. A fresh tear fell down her cheek and landed on her plate. It seemed to burst open and spread across to her sandwich, as if pointing out her betrayal to her brother.

'I'm glad you are eating something Bella, I promised your mother that I'd see that you did,' continued Tricia. 'It's one less worry for her. You need to eat at a time like this, to keep your strength up.'

Bella nodded again and was glad to feel the reassuring hand of her fiancé reach out and hold her hand under the table. She gave him a reassuring squeeze, almost of encouragement.

Irvine took this as a sign to tell his mum about what they had briefly talked about upstairs. He hadn't known if it would have been inappropriate. He spoke up anyway. 'Bella and I have decided to go ahead with our wedding as planned mum, we talked about cancelling it, but Paul wouldn't have wanted us to do that,' he looked at his fiancée as if for assurance. She nodded again, this time in definite encouragement. He put down his sandwich and used his free hand to enfold their hands together, as if already at the altar declaring their love for all to see. 'Paul would have made a great best man, he would have told some great tales, but now I'll choose another friend to be by my side. Though I think that Paul's spirit will be with us both, in the church.'

Bella bit her lip as she tried to control fresh tears. She knew that she would have to get used to many changes without her brother, this being the most important to her and her future husband.

'That's a lovely thought, but just concentrate on Paul's funeral. You both need to make sure he has a proper send-off. He deserves that, oh he was so young,' said Tricia as she burst into fresh tears. This set Bella off and the two women cried out, one for the loss of a brother, the other for the heartache she could not heal for her son and soon-to-be daughter-in-law. No amount of lip biting could dam this fresh flood of grief and Irvine was torn between comforting his fiancée and his mother. He sat quietly as

Bella gripped his hands tightly and he was glad that the decision had been made for him.

Chapter 12

'Away to bed now Hamish,' ordered Alison as she looked at her weary husband. He seemed to have aged about twenty years as she gazed into his sunken, hollow eyes. They looked ever so dull and all the sparkle that she'd loved in them was gone. She wondered if the twinkle of a life enjoyed would ever return to him, or her for that matter. She dreaded looking in the mirror. How she yearned to see her son's face again, alive, full of colour and fun. She'd have given anything to trade places with him, but life wasn't like that. It was horrific and unfair.

Hamish reached out and gave her a hug, he enveloped her in his arms and squeezed her tight. She returned the embrace, as if holding him could give her the strength needed for the week ahead. Her eyes were drawn over to the kitchen sink area and she was puzzled as to why

Hamish had taken the time to clean it. But then she realised that Molly must have popped in, sorted him out, made them both a cup of tea, and then left. She sighed, grateful for such a good friend and neighbour. She could see her tepid tea growing ever colder, by the kettle, but she was heartened to see that Hamish's favourite mug was empty.

Mistaking the sigh, Hamish mumbled, 'Aye lass, I know. This old body of mine needs a few hours of kip, then I can look after you and Bella. I'll be down in an hour or two.' He broke off the embrace.

Alison patted his back, 'Make that two or three, you must be shattered.'

'Aye, my days of long stags on guard duty, or days on military exercises without much sleep are long behind me,' he mumbled as he made for the stairs. He paused long enough to see his wife reach once more for the cordless house phone, still hot to the touch from the last call, despite having been on the charger base. She hadn't managed to call her relatives yet, she'd phoned both their works, to cancel shifts for the next week or so. She'd been pleasantly surprised to find that Molly had already informed their respective employers. She'd broken down on the phone at the kindness of their bosses who had told her not to even think of coming in until after the funeral and could they send flowers. All Alison could think of was what flowers should she and Hamish have in a wreath and in what shape or words should it be. '*Son,*' just didn't seem enough. How could flowers convey to the other mourners just how deep their loss was? She watched reluctantly as Hamish climbed their stairs, he was so stooped, like an elderly, infirm man struggling to get to bed. She wished that she could help him up and then curl into bed with him and die and be with their baby. She grasped the phone to give herself more resolve and made her way into the lounge.

Hamish paused at their bedroom door, then walked over to his son's room. He opened it and looked in. His eyes wandered over the posters for computer games that he didn't understand. That he couldn't play because they were too noisy and involved shooting and he'd had enough of seeing the result of gun play in real life. He'd been glad that Paul hadn't followed in his footsteps to be in the army or a nurse. His sensitive soul wasn't made for those sights. He'd thought his son would be safe from war, but now he'd left his family to struggle in the ultimate battle, grief. And they would be the losers in this emotional war.

He walked in and quietly sat on his son's unmade bed for a few moments. He looked out absently to their garden. The birds outside were chirruping away, tweeting deep in their own conversation as they bobbed and darted amongst the feeders before settling on the barren tree branches that swayed gently in the winter's breeze. Normally Hamish would draw comfort from these sounds and sights, but not today. Instead he turned away, stood up and walked over to Paul's chest of drawers. He pulled the second lowest one out, reached in for a football top and held it to his face. He breathed in the scent of his child, carefree joy and expectation that was mixed with the faded fragrance of Lynx deodorant. His final breath in choked him and he spurted out a sob with spittle and snot as he sobbed deep into the shirt as if he were holding the fallen corpse of his boy, grief-stricken at the inevitability of it all. He felt his legs buckle and he sank to his knees, the sound muffled and absorbed into the deep pile of the red carpet. He stooped over clutching the garment close to his chest and curled up into a ball, wailing out for his dead child.

Alison sat on the sofa and looked up to the family photo, taken at the local photographer's studio. They were sat on the white sheet, making them look like they were in a void landscape from Doctor Who, Paul's favourite television programme. She so wished that she had a TARDIS and could go back in time and, like in the portrait, hold onto both her children and tell them that she loved them and would keep them safe.

The phone dropped from her hands and bounced onto the carpet. The green button must have been pushed as it glanced against the sofa leg on its way down. The dial tone was now sounding its dull, constant tone, like that of a life-support machine alerting the nurses to a dead patient. She clutched her hands to her chest, as if she was having a heart-attack. Then she fell onto the sofa, lifted her legs up, drew them towards her chest and, in the foetal position, sobbed for her lost son and her devastated family, little knowing that her husband was in the same position upstairs. Neither could have been consoled had they reached out to the other.

Bella lay on the bed, feeling safe with Irvine's arms wrapped around her. She had fallen asleep holding his face. She remembered watching for his blinks, wanting to feel the warmth of his breath flowing through him. She had checked for the rise and fall of his chest. Its rhythmic flow had lulled her into a peaceful sleep. But she had awakened with a start and faced the reality of her loss. She gripped Irvine harder and he had simply held onto her, still not knowing what to do, little realising that he was doing the right thing in just being there for her.

Hamish's phone vibrated in his back pocket, its shakings and ringtone woke him from the deep sleep he had fallen into. He had cried himself to sleep and now he too had awakened to the reality of his grief.

'Hello Mr Dewart, it's Catriona here. I just wanted to let you know that our tests on Paul have finished and he can now be transferred to your choice of undertaker. There is a really sensitive one at…'

Hamish interrupted her, 'No. we'll use the local firm, I've seen lots of people thank him for his kindness in the newspaper family announcements section.'

'Oh, well okay, if you are sure, only…'

Hamish was more adamant this time, 'Aye, totally sure, I only want the best for my boy.'

'Of course, Mr Dewart and please be assured that he's had the best of care here. Our staff work closely with the local undertakers to save you any trouble. We just need

you to verbally authorise them to come and collect Paul
and take them into their care. It's almost five o'clock now,
so we shan't release him until the morning.'

'I understand lass. I'll do that now and then Paul can be
collected first thing in the morning.'

'Thank you, Mr Dewart, and if there is anything you need
from me, just let me know. I work from 10am to 5pm on
the number I gave you, except weekends, unless it is an
emergency.

'No, just make sure the bastard that killed my son pays
for it,' Hamish replied and then abruptly hung up the
phone, not trusting himself any further. He looked at the
screen, hesitated as he saw his ragged reflection in the
glass, and then pocketed the device and stood up. He
wiped his eyes and nose with the back of his sleeve and
then realising that he was still clutching Paul's shirt with
his other hand, he reverently placed it, sodden, back in the

opened drawer. He closed it gently and walked out of the room, closing the door quietly behind him. He made his way downstairs.

Alison, upon hearing his footsteps, sat up and then bent forward and picked up the house phone. She hit the red button and switched off the continual ringtone. She quickly took out a wet tissue from her pocket and wiped her eyes and nose. She inhaled sharply to stop the flow of snot from her nose. It tasted vile as she involuntarily took a swallow. She stood up with more resolve than she really felt and walked out of the lounge. Hamish was just coming out of the bathroom, where she knew he had been washing his face so that she would not see his tears. She hoped that hers would not show and further upset him.

They reached out their hands and connected like two lovers reunited at a train station, reaching through the barrier that separated passenger from expectant onlooker. Their touch was all that was needed and conveyed so much information to each other through their long years of marriage.

Hamish did not ask his wife how she was, he could see how she was. Instead he stated, 'That was the police liaison officer, they have finished their tests and Paul can be released. He'll have to stay at the mortuary tonight though. The staff only deal with emergencies after 5pm.'

Alison merely nodded, what words could convey how she felt. She wanted her son home, and in his room, playing games with his mates and being rowdy. She hated the empty silence that hung in the air like the grim reaper's scythe that had then cut through the heart of her family.

Hamish squeezed her hand in agreement, though no words had been said. He too hated the thought of his son being alone in the fridge at the morgue. Or worse still, being stored amongst strangers, united in the cold and their stillness.

'I'm going to phone the undertakers now, the local chaps, I bet they won't knock off until after six, they open their resting rooms in the evenings for families to view their loved ones.' He looked down to see the cordless home phone in her hand. 'I'll go through to the kitchen and use my mobile. I'll look up their website and get their phone number. You sit down lass and phone your pals. You'll need them.'

'I haven't phoned my sisters yet,' mumbled Alison, weakly.

'Ah,' replied Hamish, wondering if she'd just crumpled into a ball and wept, like he had. 'How about you do that whilst I phone the undertaker and then make us a cup of tea, can you manage that love?'

'Yes, I'll just sit down,' replied Alison as she shuffled through to the lounge.

Hamish watched her go and then reached into his back pocket for his mobile and made his way through the kitchen as he typed away on the search engine. He flicked through to the contact us page and once he saw the phone number, he tapped the screen and it automatically dialled for him.

Alison closed the lounge door and then wearily sat down on the sofa again. This time she relaxed into its soft cushions and then with a sigh, she dialled her oldest sister, Emma's, number. She had rehearsed what she would say to Paul's favourite aunty but when she heard, 'Hello Alison,' in the headset she crumpled and fell into fresh tears and sobbed.

'Hello, is that Green's, the undertaker,' asked Hamish.

'Yes, it is,' replied an elderly voice, 'How may I help you.'

'I'm afraid my son died this morning, in a road traffic accident, by a drunk driver, he was shunted off the road.'

There was a sharp intake of breath at the other end of the telephone. Then a composed voice said gently, 'Oh, I'm so sorry to hear that Mr…'

'Dewart, but please call me Hamish.'

'I'm so sorry for your loss Hamish. Would you like us, I have my son helping me these days, he's going to take over the firm when I retire next year,' his voice tailed off for a few seconds and Hamish waited patiently for him to retrieve his train of thought. 'Sorry about that, it's been an eventful day. Ah yes, shall we take your boy into our care and would you like us to arrange the funeral?'

'Yes please,' replied Hamish, though he wondered if the old boy was up to it. He hadn't realised that he was near retirement age.

'Well don't you worry about a thing, we'll take good care of...'

'Paul, his name is, was, Paul.'

There was another sharp intake of breath and Hamish wondered if perhaps he had to retire due to some sort of respiratory disease.

'I'm assuming that Paul is currently resting at Queen Street in Aberdeen?'

Hamish couldn't resist a small smile at the gentle terminology used by this profession. He'd phoned enough of them when he'd nursed terminal patients and they had to be taken from the nursing home in their grey or black body bags that glided easily from bed to their collapsible trolley and into their unmarked black vans. 'Yes, though they said he wouldn't be able to be collected until the morning.'

'Don't you worry about a thing Hamish, we'll take good care of Paul. I've got to go into Aberdeen this evening anyway. I'll phone the staff there and have a word with them. We know them well, as you can imagine, we are there quite often. They'll have been told to expect me. I'll sign Paul over to our care. He'll get our special treatment; don't you worry about a thing. When you are ready, come into the office after ten in the morning and we'll go through the arrangements.'

'Thank you, Mr Green,' replied Hamish, grateful for someone to shoulder some of his heavy burden.

'It'll be my pleasure Hamish,' acknowledged the undertaker.

Chapter 13

'Oh love, it's just so appalling, let me come over, I'll bring Hector, he can take Hamish out for a pint,' insisted Emma. 'I'll fetch something out of the freezer to reheat for you both. I expect you both need a good meal.'

'Oh, I'd love that,' sighed Alison to her sister. She was now composed and had cried down the phone for a good few minutes whilst her sister nervously waited on the other end, not knowing what to make of her sister's distress. Emma had thought that perhaps Hamish had left her or had revealed that he'd had an affair. She hadn't expected this devastating news. She was shocked, but knew she had to keep calm for her younger sister's sake. 'But I've still got to tell the rest of the family,' continued Alison, 'I need to tell them. Then I need to phone our friends, and those of

Paul's. Though I think I'll leave them till last as I think Bella will be doing that. She's still at Irvine's. Oh…'

'Oh Alison, your poor Paul, and poor Bella and Hamish, and you. Oh, I just don't know what to say, or what to do. Paul was far too young. He was so full of life, we always had fun with him. Hector loved his company. Let me be there for you,' Emma persisted, the older sister role coming to the fore.

Alison toyed with this idea, but sighed with how tired she felt, 'No, I'll need you tomorrow, after we've been to the undertakers. I just want to take another of Hamish's pills and then fall asleep,' she omitted to add that she felt like not wanting to wake up.

'Okay sis, but you just phone, no matter what the time is, we'll be there for you both. Please give Bella and Hamish our love too. Tomorrow I'm bringing lunch and tea, I insist,' said Emma, though she didn't know that Molly would be heavily defending her right to do so too and was already preparing her famous stew.

'I will, love you too.' Alison then hung up the phone, not trusting her emotions, for the tears were never far away and with each person she told of Paul's death, it was like she'd been told the grim news by the police all over again.

Monique kicked off her white rubber shoes and they bounced around the bottom of her locker with an echo like a spanner wielding submariner testing the hulk of his boat against the might of the ocean. She then slipped off her green scrubs, bundled them up, and then threw them into the nearby laundry trolley with the ease of a professional basketball player. She shuffled about, as if shaking off the dead skin and dust from her charges and then reached across to her coconut moisturiser and liberally applied some all over her body, paying special attention to her hands, arms and face. She found this scented lotion to be the only remedy that worked against the mortuary smell that followed her around like a dull cloud. She couldn't wait to see her lover and have a fun night. Tomorrow's post-mortems could wait, she was off duty now and could leave the morgue to the tender care of her assistant. She slipped on her jeans, pullover and then finally her heels, closed her locker and left the changing-room, making her way to the nearest bar.

Catriona momentarily toyed with her Glen Garioch, allowing the whisky to caress the inside of the glass like a seductive massage. She took the glass to her lips, teased it there for the briefest of moments and then cradled it under her nose. She took a steady sniff as the spirit's vapours released their tempting flavours and entered her nasal passage and flowed through her, urging her to yield to temptation and take a sip. She obliged. Only she didn't just take a small amount, she downed the single measure, neat in the glass, no ice-cubes or drop of mineral water to help release the subtle earthy fruity flavours.

'Rough day!' joked the barman upon seeing one of his regulars, and a good tipper, down the measure that he'd poured only seconds ago.

'Oh yes!' understated Catriona. 'But that's made it go a bit smoother, until the morning, when I have to do it all over again,' she sighed.

'I know the feeling, welcome to the rat race.' He nodded to the empty glass, 'a refill?' he offered, hoping for another tip.

'Better not, my date hates it when I smell of booze.' She popped a mint into her mouth and toyed with it as if to release its flavours. She hated herself for this deception.

The barman looked crestfallen, unseen by the police officer. 'But I'll have a soft drink, what'll perk me up?'

The barman looked happy, a free drink was about to come his way. 'How about a pear and elderflower lemonade? It's refreshing on the palate, especially if you are about to eat.'

Catriona smiled, gave a small bow of her head, as if to acknowledge the expertise of the professional before her, and said, 'That sounds suitably fruity and pert! I'll have one of those please, and one for yourself.' She handed over a fiver, not expecting any change.

The barman smiled, 'That's kind, thank you. I'll get that right away. Ice in it?'

Catriona involuntarily shivered, she thought about the biting cold day and how chilly the mortuary had been. 'No thanks, I've been cold all day.'

The barman, ever the clever salesman, nodded to their specials board, 'That'll warm you up, our famous Illicit Still ale battered fish and chips.'

Catriona smiled fondly, that was her favourite meal whenever they dined here. The barman had a face she knew well. But it was now too late to ask his name, for she'd been coming here for years, ever since transferring to the Aberdeen police from Dundee. He knew her well enough; she loved the chips the most, the chef cleverly left the skins on the potatoes and sliced them up thick. They were lovely and hearty and with a generous crunch. Real comfort food, she unconsciously rubbed her stomach, and was glad not to have the thickening waistline that befell her deskbound peers. Taking the stairs up and down to the morgue, instead of the lift, helped her to burn off those indulgent calories. 'It certainly will, we'll be eating soon, and I can't wait.'

The barman smiled, placed her drink on the bar and retreated tactfully to the optics, busying himself looking busy.

Catriona took a long gulp of her drink, the bubbles worked their way from her empty stomach back up and through to her nose, lingering a short spell to engage with the previous whisky and struck out with a small belch. 'Oh,' she said in embarrassment, 'that's a really tasty drink thanks for the suggestion.'

The barman smiled towards her and continued polishing the optics. Ever the professional, he ignored her burping sounds so as not to embarrass his best tipper.

Catriona looked around her, loving the historic feel of this building that was said to be one of the last criminal haunts of bootleggers who were hiding their whisky cache from the excisemen. It was ironic that it was now the local watering hole of the police force whose headquarters could be seen, one street away. Few modern-day criminals set foot in here once they knew who frequented the building. There were few pub brawls and disturbances here, even when sports events such as the football was broadcast on their huge screens and much ale was drunk by all. She could hear the clip, clopping from the stairs, even above the sound of the music. She smiled.

The door opened, and Monique strolled in, the faint aroma of coconut wafting in, seductive and alluring, like the thought of a tempting beach holiday in warmer climates. She smiled as she spied Catriona by the bar, and she walked over.

Catriona stood up from her bar stool and took a step forward to greet her. They kissed full on the lips and Monique gave a gentle, playful dart of her tongue as she held her lover close. '*Oh dear, I can taste whisky,*' she thought. They unclenched from their embrace, the others in the bar giving them no heed. Aberdonians felt liberated and carefree, now that they'd had their first Gay Pride event endorsed by the Council. This was now a commonplace greeting across the city. 'Have you had a good day?' asked Monique, dreading the inevitable reply.

'No, not really. As you know I've had quite a few families to process, bless them, some were stoical, but others just wept and wailed. You can never tell how they are going to react when I take them downstairs and then pull aside that curtain. It's not a Ta Da! moment,' replied Catriona. She took a sip of her fruity lemonade in the hope that it would disguise the smell of her whisky. She didn't know that the cat was already out of the bag.

'Oh dear,' replied Monique, trying to look sympathetic, 'but I know you, I know that you are the right person for this job, you've got such sympathy and can talk to the families in such an empathetic way. You'll bring them such comfort without realising it, so much better than someone with size eleven boots. You are made for the job, you can listen and convey information with such sensitivity. Give it another month or so Catriona.'

'I don't know if I can, it's the sights too, when I pulled back the wrong sheet and saw, and saw,' she stuttered as she recalled what was underneath. 'I mean, blimey, how do you even begin to touch that, and look and examine?' she asked as she shuddered at the memory.

'Och, you just get used to it. I rarely deal with the families directly, so I don't have an emotional charge or connection. I still feel for the person whose body it once was. I'm not like Martin, who has a religious faith, but I do respect what was once their vessel. Though I don't say a silent prayer like Martin does every time he picks up his scalpel. That brief minute as he is poised over the body probably allows him to focus his thoughts as he prays for the departed soul. I kind of pause too, but really to think about how I am going to help gather evidence for a possible trial, or to find a cause of death that might bring some sort of solace to a family. And your job is just as important, because you sensitively tell a family a cause of death, let them know that their loved one did not suffer, and that in some cases the perpetrator will get punished. You have to convey hope and a sense of justice in their darkest of hours.'

'Aye, maybe, but Jesus, the mess that was under that sheet…'

'Is still a human being,' interrupted Monique, 'though in the case of the man that killed those two and then took a running jump off the balcony, well, I'm not sure he deserves to be called that. But I still have a job to do and I'll continue to do it to the best of my ability, as should you.'

The barman saw a good jumping in point. He had casually listened into the conversation and had been feeling a bit perturbed about the subject matter, spoken so freely at his pristine bar. He smiled at Monique and asked, can I get you a drink?'

'Oh, yes please, it's been a long day,' she looked to Catriona as she said, 'how about a glass each of Sauvignon Blanc?'

Catriona nodded, and Monique could see how moist her eyes had become. She turned back to the barman, 'So much for our dry January! You'd better make that the bottle and two glasses, and could you please take it to the table over there along with two menus?' She pointed to a discrete table in the corner where she could console Catriona. She took out her purse and slipped out three ten-pound notes. 'And please keep the change.'

The barman smiled, 'No problem at all ladies, I do recommend the fish.' Being a Monday, the chef had told him to try and offload the weekend's produce before it turned.

'Great idea,' replied Monique enthusiastically, 'some warming, comforting food for us both?' she turned back to Catriona and nodded.

Catriona smiled, she loved those chips, 'Yes please, two specials would be perfect.'

The barman smiled, *'what perfect customers these are,'* he thought, 'You both go and make yourself comfortable and I'll inform chef and bring your drinks over.'

Alison hesitated at the lounge door, she could hear Hamish on his mobile and didn't want to disturb him. She returned to the sofa and sank back, though she could not feel relaxed, she doubted that she ever would. She looked up at the smiling photo of her son and sighed. She hoped that wherever he was, that he would be at peace. She began to talk to him.

'Thank you, Douglas. It would be great to see you. I think it'll do me the world of good to have a brisk walk and talk with you in the morning. And take some of your pigeons, you can race them home. I love seeing them fly out of your basket and then regroup in the sky before flying off. Alright, see you in the morning. Bye,' said Hamish as he hung up on his best friend. He'd need the strength from his pal so that he could be there for his girls. He smiled, despite himself. Whenever Douglas drove up from Aberdeen, he always took his prized pigeons with him, and wherever they parked his car, he'd release them after their walk and hope to be home before them. He never was. He'd describe how he'd go through to his back garden, and they'd always be perched on the shed roof, waiting to go inside, through the special one-way system that he called a sputnik trap. Once he'd opened the hatch, they'd pop in and go straight to the feeders or water. He'd explained how his pigeons had been a quiet distraction after his wife had died. He'd spend hours with them, watching their gentle head bobbing and listen to their peaceful cooing. If anyone understood grief, it would be his dear pal Douglas.

Hamish walked through from the kitchen and paused at the lounge door. Through the glass pane he could see his wife looking up at the family portrait and she looked as if she was talking to it. He paused at the door, allowing her to finish her conversation. He wondered what she was saying to Paul.

Monique raised her glass to Catriona's, smiled and said, 'Cheers my dear,' hoping to lighten the mood.

Catriona clinked glasses and returned the cheers, but her eyes lacked a sparkle. She glugged the wine and enjoyed the freeing sensation as it worked its magic, relaxing her. She sat back in her seat and sighed. 'Okay, I'll give it a few more weeks. The thought of being able to see more of you during the day is the only benefit of the job. Even that is few and far between.'

'Ah, but isn't it fun, grabbing an illicit kiss here and there!' Monique pondered on what she said, 'Ha, how appropriate, we're in the Illicit Still, I bet the old moonshiners would have had a fit if they'd have known that one day the police and a pathologist would be drinking here!'

Catriona laughed, 'and two same sex lovers!' she exclaimed with a gleam in her eye.

'*That's my girl*!' thought Monique, '*She's back*!' Caught up in the mood she reached over to high-five her lover and was delighted to see it returned enthusiastically. She was pleased that her prescription of wine had been the right medicine. She leant over and whispered, 'How about I run you a nice candle-lit bath when we get home and you can try out that Cheer Up Buttercup bath-bomb I bought you from Lush?'

Catriona smiled, and coyly said, 'And how about you join me!'

The barman discretely waited at the bar for a few more seconds before grinning and taking their fish and chips over.

Alison reluctantly turned away from the photo and was about to stand up when Hamish took his cue and opened the lounge door. 'Who was that you were talking too Hamish, was it the undertaker? Is he collecting Paul in the morning?' she asked.

'No lass, the undertaker is collecting Paul this evening. It was Mr Green himself, the old boy, he's in Aberdeen collecting his son, so he's kindly going to collect Paul, so you don't have to worry about him being on his own in the morgue. I didn't realise they run things on a 24-hour basis. He'll be comfortable in one of their rest rooms and then we can see him in the morning, you know, when they've, em…' floundered Hamish as he sat down by his wife.

She reached over and patted her husband's hands before taking them in hers. 'I know what needs to be done to our Paul,' she simply stated.

Hamish gave her hands a loving squeeze and quickly changed the subject, 'I also gave Douglas a call. We are going for a quick walk in the morning, at about seven, so you stay in bed and I'll fetch something from the bakery to fortify us for the day ahead.'

'Och, I doubt I'll sleep Hamish.'

'Aye, you will lass, I think you should take another of my pills.'

Alison nodded and then remembered, 'He'll be taking his pigeons?'

'Aye lass,' Hamish smiled, 'though I doubt he'll beat them home.'

Alison gave the briefest of smiles, 'And what about Scott, how is his father going to break it to him? Scott loved playing with Paul, he treated him like a little brother.'

'Scott's still on tour, Operation Trenton I think he called it. He's in South Sudan again, providing humanitarian medical care. Douglas thought it best to wait until he's home from leave. If Scott goes to Aldershot to see his new girlfriend, then Douglas is going to drive down and break the news himself. I'm afraid he won't be able to come to the funeral or get compassionate leave as Paul wasn't a direct next of kin.'

Alison nodded, remembering the bureaucracy of the military. 'Best not to upset Scott more than is needed. I know he'd have liked to have paid his respects if he could.'

Hamish nodded, 'I know he'll come and see us when he's next home on leave and in Aberdeen. It sounds like he's met a lovely lass. She has a small boy.'

They both looked up at their son's photo, each lost in their own thoughts.

Chapter 14

'Do you think they'll mind?' asked Bella as she snuggled into her fiancée.

Irvine reached around her and drew her in tighter and cradled her in his arms. They were on his bed, each drawing in comfort from the other. Bella had cried all her tears as he silently held on to her. 'I think they'll be fine, they have each other and I've never seen a more loving couple than your mum and dad. They'll be there for each other and happy that you are safe and well. But you should call them and tell them what you are going to do. You don't want them worrying about you.'

Bella reluctantly broke off the embrace and sat up. She yawned and stretched. 'I feel so tired. I think it was all the crying.'

'Yes, that'll make you sleepy. I'll have to warn you that mum is making you one of her hot chocolates. She told me earlier when you were in the toilet that I mustn't let you leave without drinking it. She's probably fluffing up the mini marshmallows as I speak! You take my mobile from the bedside cabinet and phone your mum and I'll let mine know that you are staying.' He looked at his watch. 'She'll be pleased that you are staying for dinner. She's probably cooked enough for all of us anyway.' He too sat up and gave a small stretch, to reawaken his limbs that had gone to sleep that his soon-to-be-wife had been lying on. He then opened his bedroom door and went downstairs.

Bella reached for Irvine's mobile phone and dialled home.

The house cordless phone called out its uplifting musical tone, but neither of the listeners were feeling upbeat.

Alison let go of her husband's hands and reached for the phone. Looking at the caller display she said to her husband, 'That's Bella, she's probably ready to be collected.'

Hamish stood up and gave Paul's photo another look, and then made his way to their lobby, where he pulled down his coat from the hooks. As he pulled it on, he heard his wife say, 'Okay, I'll tell your dad.' He went back into the lounge and waited patiently for Alison to finish her call with an 'I love you too.'

'Is she okay?' asked Hamish.

'Yes, she wants to stay overnight. Irvine will take her home in the morning.'

'Okay,' replied Hamish, shrugging off his jacket, 'so long as she is safe.' He returned into the lobby and popped his jacket back on its hook. He lingered there for a while, absently stroking Paul's summer jacket. He wondered

246

what was the correct thing to do with Paul's things that were scattered around the house? Should he be removing things such as his toothbrush and razor?

His thoughts were interrupted by his wife calling through, 'Are you still there love?'

Hamish snapped out of his reverie and returned to the lounge,' Aye, just a bit tired. I pray that we never have another day like today.'

Alison nodded and looked at the time. 'I know it's only eight o' clock but I'm shattered. I've rung all the folk I can think of that needs to know about our Paul. Should we go to bed early and try and get some sleep?'

'That's a good idea lass, why don't you go and get yourself ready for bed and I'll lock up for the night.'

Alison stood up from the sofa, gave the family portrait one last look and left the room saying, 'I'll take a glass of water up and I think we both should take your pills, to help us sleep and prepare ourselves for tomorrow.'

Hamish nodded and followed his wife through to their kitchen where he checked the back door was locked. He deliberately didn't put the chain on the door, for he knew Molly would very likely be up with the larks, trying to get them to eat breakfast. Though a man of great appetite, he'd lost it after today's events and couldn't face eating again. He walked back through to the lobby and checked that the front door was locked. He did not bother with this chain either. Neither of his children were home, and though he knew the answer, he left it unchained in case Bella changed her mind and returned home. He knew that Paul would never return to them. He sighed deeply as he made his way to the bathroom. There was no sign of Alison, she'd already climbed the stairs. He hesitated at the lounge and then opened the door and made his way in. He didn't bother with the light switch and instead relied on the dim light from the hallway that cast itself into the room, like a fading, wandering, lighthouse's beam. He walked over to the family portrait, the light appearing to shine on Paul's face, like a spotlight in a theatre highlighting an actor. 'Goodnight son, wherever you are.'

The black, nondescript van reversed into the loading bay area at the back of the police headquarters, near to the ramped area. The driver left a few metres space behind him as he applied the brakes and shut the engine down. Silence filled the area until an elderly figure, in a grey three-piece suit opened the van door and slowly, and with apparent effort, opened both doors at the back of the vehicle. He tugged at a metal handled object within and a collapsible trolley broke free and glided down onto the concrete floor. He reached in and found a purple velvety like drape and flung it onto the trolley. He left the doors open, exposing the two shelved areas with reinforced metal brackets. There was room for two. Though most would not choose to travel this way. He then made his way to the ramp. He gratefully ignored the stairs, as he wheezed and coughed with this effort of pushing his trolley. He stopped midway and reached into his pocket and withdrew his inhaler and took two quick puffs and then pocketed it, where it nestled snugly with his crumpled packet of Benson & Hedges. A door creaked open for want of a drop of oil. A figure in green scrubs emerged and smiled. 'Have you not got Flinn to help you Brendan?'

Mr Green, the undertaker, smiled back, his yellow teeth reflecting dully in the subdued lighting. 'No. I'm collecting him in a minute.'

The assistant nodded, knowing when to keep quiet in this man's presence.

Mr Green reached into his pocket and took out a fold of twenty-pound notes. He peeled three off, hesitated, and then took out another two, pocketing the remainder. He walked closer to the mortuary assistant and handed them over, secure in the knowledge that this area was the CCTV blind spot. 'Thanks for staying behind. Shall we get Paul loaded up?'

The assistant took the notes and crumpled them into his fist, his scrubs were like shrouds, they had no pockets. Only, unlike a corpse, he could take this new wealth with him. He carefully carried the money in his hands until he could get to his locker. He'd be spending his money wisely tonight, at the Pittodrie Bar as he made his way home to his single-roomed flat in King Street, just across from the new student accommodation. He'd be meeting one of them tonight for an A-Bomb. The flats were a handy place to meet his supplier. They provided a purer hit, but this marijuana and heroin cigarette came at a heavy price, in cost and to his health. He curled his notes all the tighter at the thought of taking a relaxing drag. 'Aye, nae bother, are you sure you'll be fine taking the strain of the trolley down the ramp?'

'I'm not in my grave yet,' growled Brendan as he coughed up some phlegm and spat it onto the concrete flooring. 'Let's get inside and sort out the paperwork and get loaded up. I don't want to keep my son waiting.'

The assistant turned without acknowledging the undertaker's quick temper. He wanted to keep him sweet as the backhanders paid for his drinks and drugs most nights. It was worth the few hours waiting in solitude for the old swine to turn up so that the undertaker could boast a 24-hour service to his customers. They certainly paid highly for it in return. Besides, he quite enjoyed the peaceful silence of the morgue after the day's noisy whirring of saws, washing down of tables and hustle and bustle of police, Procurator Fiscal staff and the stuck-up boss. Though he didn't mind the pert Monique, she was good fun and easy on the eye. He broke off his thoughts and said, 'He's out of the fridge and all wrapped up, ready for your checks and transfer to your trolley,' replied the assistant as he held onto the bank notes through his puffy fingers. He was becoming as bloated as a corpse fished out of Aberdeen's harbour, but would not go to see his GP, despite the boss urging him to make an appointment. He was fine, he just needed a drink and another hit, besides, today was a busy and eventful day that'll keep the detectives in work for a few weeks.

'Good,' wheezed Brendan, unaware of the assistant's growing health problem that he was funding. Though the undertaker's wheezing was becoming more apparent to the morgue attendant who worried that his cash cow may stop producing milk.

They reached the row of fridges, the faint hum of electric fans giving out an auditory reassurance that the corpses within were keeping as fresh as possible. The assistant handed the undertaker a sheaf of papers which he accepted in his withered hand with a snatch worthy of a tag player.

Mr Green carefully read through the transfer notes, took out his pen and quickly scribbled his signature in the relevant sections. An act he'd done countless times over the years. He walked over to the morgue's trolley, bent down and whipped off the sheet, as if quickly stripping a bed. He threw it onto the floor with careless abandon. He cast aside his own purple velvet drape from his trolley and then he looked down at Paul, his arms were straight down his body, as if he was lying to attention. There was not a mark on him, except to the face where there were plenty of laceration scars. The Y scar was done at the post-mortem. He must have suffered though as he went flying through his windscreen. He looked puzzled, as if working out why his seatbelt and airbag had not saved him. That'll be one for the forensics and detectives to work out, in the workshop that filled the basement area next door. He pulled his trolley closer to the morgue trolley and pushed down with his foot on the pedal to apply its brakes. He checked that the brakes were on the other and took a hold of Paul's legs. He nodded to Paul's upper torso and the assistant obliged.

'On three,' advised Mr Green and once he'd counted, they glided Paul across onto the hard-metallic surface of his smaller trolley. He picked up his purple blanket and flung it over Paul, its carefully weighted edges would stop it fluttering in tonight's now gentle breeze. It completely covered Paul, as if deliberately covering up the crime of the drunk-driver. He grasped the metal handle of the foot

end and said, 'He'll be going in the lower section of the

van,' and pulled at the trolley, yearning to take another

puff on his inhaler, but not wanting to show his health

problem to this man. He breathlessly walked back to the

van, allowing the assistant to make all the pushing effort,

and then letting him take the strain as they wheeled Paul

down the ramp and into the back of the black van with no

livery or markings, though most people knew this to be a

private ambulance for those already heaven-bound. The

assistant clutched the bank notes all the tighter in case the

undertaker sought a refund. He needn't have worried, he

was already closing the back doors and hobbling off to the

driver's door without a backward glance, or a thank you.

The assistant scurried off with his reward.

Hamish paused at the door of their bedroom. He could hear whimpering, not from within, but from Paul's bedroom. He walked over to his door and hesitated. *'Would it always be Paul's room, kept as a shrine, like on those television programs where mother's proudly say that it's as it was on the day their child was snatched away from them. Or would it become a guest room for visitors to stay overnight?'* he grimly thought. *'So many forced changes to their happy home and happy life.'* He hesitated at his son's room and wondered if he should go in. He came to a decision and did so and saw the sight that he had expected. Curled up in Paul's bed was Alison, in the foetal position, clutching at Paul's favourite t-shirt, crying into it as he had done earlier. He turned around and strode off to their bedroom and pulled the duvet from their bed and returned to his distraught wife. He pulled a generous amount of the duvet over her, then climbed into the bed and spooned his wife whilst covering the remainder of the duvet over himself. He had no words of comfort, for there were none for either of them. Instead he simply held her until they passed the time in which the police had previously knocked on their door. They had got through one day without their beloved son, and each would try and get through another, for the sake of their daughter. Then they would repeat the procedure as if muscle-memory were guiding them through. Each had run out of tears, and despite not taking his sleeping pills, each dozed fitfully through the night, coming to frightful starts and remembering that this had been no dream, but was a living nightmare of their worst terrors.

Chapter 15

The doorbell resounded around the house until it penetrated through to the dozing ears of Hamish. He heard the gentle patter of feet downstairs and in his half-awakened state, he wondered if Bella had come home. He looked to his son's digital clock on the bedside table, it was five minutes past seven. It was too early for visitors to come and pay their respects. Then he heard subdued voices and remembered, it would be Douglas. And it sounded like Molly too. She must have had an early night as well. He sniffed the air, Yes, it was unmistakeably the smell of bacon being cooked. His belly involuntarily rumbled in appreciation and anticipation. He gently slipped his arms from around Alison and moved out of bed. He looked down and was surprised to see that he was fully dressed. He slipped on his slippers. Hamish looked across at Alison and saw that she was fully dressed too, and still clutching Paul's t-shirt. Despite their grief, they had fallen asleep. He pulled the duvet back over her and quietly left his son's room. As he went down the stairs, he heard muffled conversation that grew more distinct with every step.

'It was kind of expected that I'd lose Bill, he was in his early seventies, but if your Scott's now in the army, then you must have been so young to lose your wife.'

'Oh aye, bless her, Rhona was in her early thirties and our Scott was still in primary school. That's what made him want to be a nurse. A male nurse really looked after him whenever I visited the hospice. He'd take the time to take Scott away and make him toast and chat away with him while I had some time alone with Rhona. And when she died, he made sure that Scott held his mum's hand and kissed her. I wasn't in a fit state to think clearly and know what was best for our boy.' Douglas smiled at the thought of his wife and son and then asked Molly, 'So Hamish cared for Bill in his last days?'

'Oh yes. Him and Alison. Bill wanted to die at home you see. The hospice arranged for him to come home. They even organised for a special bed to be delivered. He was much more comfortable in that, during his final days. So, in between nurses and carers visits, Hamish and Alison would take turns making sure he was comfortable. I owe a lot to them.'

Douglas looked across to the frying pan and piles of cut up and buttered rolls. 'It looks like you're taking good care of them now.'

'She certainly is,' joined in Hamish as he entered the kitchen.

Douglas rose and wrapped his arms around his friend and drew him in for a tight embrace. 'I'm so sorry Hamish, no son should go before his father. It's not the right order of things and it's not fair what happened to Paul. How are you bearing up?'

'Well, you know,' replied Hamish.

'No, but I have a fair idea. I felt so numb and shocked when my Rhona died. And I knew it was coming. The cancer left her the shell of the woman I loved. But I had time to say goodbye and tell her that I loved her and that I would look after our son,' Douglas hesitated, not sure if he was saying the right things, 'but your poor Paul.' He placed his hand on Hamish's shoulder and patted it twice. 'Scott loved him like a wee brother. He always asked after him whenever I went to Aldershot to visit him.'

'I'm pleased you are here Douglas, thank you for coming all this way, and so early too. Shall we be going for our walk now? I thought we'd go around the path to the lighthouse. It should be quiet at this time of the day.'

'Not before you both eat one of these,' interrupted Molly as she held two plates of bacon rolls out, the meat still appearing to sizzle in the buns. They were crispy and covered in brown sauce, just as Hamish liked them. She nodded to the kitchen table.

'I think it best that we do as we are told mate,' laughed Douglas.

Molly nodded, 'I can see that we are going to get along fine Douglas,' she grinned as she felt the plates being taken from her grasp. The two men sat down at the kitchen table and ate in companionable silence.

Bella stirred in her sleep, moaned out in protest to a nightmare, and settled back into her fitful slumber. Irvine reached up and stroked her hair with small, slow strokes of pacification. He had dozed through the night, trying to placate her with every fresh wave of grief that burst through her like an unwelcome tidal wave of emotion. He still wasn't sure about what to say, or what to do. He had phoned his work last night and told them that he would not be in today. He needed to be there for Bella, though he had to admit to himself that he was a bit frightened about seeing Paul. He had never seen a dead body before and didn't know what to expect. Would his pal look awful? Would he be able to stomach the sight, especially as Paul had been thrown out of his car? He continued his gentle stroking of Bella's hair, more to comfort himself now if he was being honest with himself.

The red and white painted exterior of the lighthouse shone out of the early morning mist like a beacon of hope to the two walkers. The tall bricked building stood firm against the elements, anchored steadfast against any storm. It went unheeded, nothing could comfort the man whose shoulders sagged as he walked, despite his swift steps. The other carried a small cardboard box by its handles, it looked like the kind that supermarkets offered wine buyers. Only this one was fully enclosed except for the airholes dotted along the sides. The walkers wore heavy jackets against the winter morning. They were striding briskly across the bridge, the pace set by the taller of the two, despite his drooped posture. 'I don't know what to say Hamish, but you know that you can call me at any time,' stated Douglas.

'Aye, and thanks for that, it's good to know and thank you for coming, it gave me an excuse to get out in the fresh air.'

'Anytime, I really mean it, day or night. I'll make sure I get time off for Paul's funeral too, the control room will function fine without me. I mind when my Rhona passed on, you were a great pal to me. You stopped me from turning into myself. You saved Scott and I.'

'Och, that's what mates are for, but this…' Hamish stumbled for words, though his stride was firm, as if walking fast would heal his spirit and put his demons behind him.

'Aye, it's something else,' agreed his pal, though no words had been needed from the grieving father. 'You'll need your pals and family around you at a time like this. And make sure you ask. There's no shame in it. Don't be like you were when your army days caught up with you.'

'No,' stated Hamish firmly as they left the tarmac of the bridge and walked along the well-trodden path around the lighthouse. Years of dog walking by numerous villagers had carved this path out of the grassed area where rocks jutted out at irregular intervals, ready to trip unsuspecting passers-by. 'I've learnt my lesson there, just like your Scott has had to do. I take care of myself as best as I can.'

'That's good to hear,' replied Douglas as he pointed to some rocks. 'Let's sit there and you can have some Rory time!'

Hamish walked over to the large granite blocks and sat down with his friend.

Douglas, pleased for the break in the brisk exercise, opened his cardboard box and carefully took out his prized racing pigeon. It gently cooed as its head bobbed from side to side, trying to work out where it was. He passed the bird over to his pal, who took it and tenderly cradled it in his palms, 'Hello old friend,' he said soothingly to him. 'You've a long flight ahead of you.' Rory cooed as if in acknowledgement. Hamish stroked the bird with his free thumbs, taking comfort in its soft plumage and the warmth radiating from its plump breasts. The two men sat in companionable silence for a few minutes, nodding in greeting to the passing dog owner whose pet had bounded down the hill, towards the rock pools that surrounded the lighthouse. The black Labrador was in search of seals to chase. Finding none, it contented itself with splashing about in the little water that the tide had brought in. A whistle from its owner caused him to interrupt his play and return to his master. The two friends sat and watched them disappear around the bend.

'I loved Paul very much, you know,' stated Hamish.

'And he knew it and loved you very much. You were, and still are, a loving, happy family,' acknowledged Douglas.

'The bastard that shunted him was drunk,' said Hamish. Spittle flew from his lips as he fought to contain his rage. 'If I could get hold of him, I'd tear him from limb to limb.'

Douglas looked momentarily astonished at his friend's revelation and angry outburst. He inwardly processed the information and eventually replied, 'As would any father, it's a natural feeling, but for the sake of your wife and daughter, you need to acknowledge these feelings and then put them to one side.' Douglas patted the granite boulder they were using as a makeshift seat. 'You must be their rock.'

Hamish sighed as several lonely tears fell from his face and onto Rory. The bird swivelled his head in surprise and tried to flap its wings in protest, but Hamish had a good grip on him. He continued his gentle stroking of the bird and both were soon calm again. 'I saw him,' he said eventually.

'Who Paul?' gently asked a confused Douglas.

'Yes, but also the drunk driver. I drove to the accident and saw the drunk driver in the back of the ambulance.'

'Oh,' said a surprised Douglas, 'Did you get a good look at him.'

Hamish's eyes narrowed at the memory. 'Aye, but his face was covered in blood. He must have hit it on the steering wheel. He'd not been drunk enough to forget his seat belt.' His eyes narrowed further, 'I don't know why Paul hadn't been wearing his?' He left the question hanging in the air for a few moments. It remained unanswered, for Douglas could find no reply to soothe his troubled friend. 'But the bastard looked familiar, even with all the blood covering him. I just can't place him.'

Alison reached out behind her and felt the emptiness of the bed and couldn't help but compare it to the hollowness of her heart. A huge chunk of her was missing and could never be replaced. She rolled back into a foetal-like ball and clutched Paul's t-shirt tighter to her chest and wailed out against the injustice of her loss and her powerlessness to bring him back.

Molly wrung out the dishcloth tighter as her neighbour and friend howled her rage upstairs. Though she missed her Bill, it would be as nothing to the heartache that Alison would have for the rest of her life. She looked up and stared out of the kitchen window, watching the rhythmic movement of the barren tree branches as they swayed gently in the wind. Life moved on, despite sorrow, people had to go forward with their lives. Nothing stopped for grief. She filled the kettle, closed the tap and walked the few steps to the plug socket and switched on the kettle. Then she walked to the kitchen table, sat down and waited patiently.

'They'll need you now mate,' stated Douglas, looking discretely at his watch, 'It's time to let Rory off.'

Hamish nodded. They had sat in silence for a good ten minutes, looking out to sea. Hamish had lost himself watching the ebb and flow of the ocean batter against the rocks. Its rhythmic movement had lulled him into a peace of sorts and had helped to dissipate his anger. 'See you later old boy,' he snuggled his nose up close to the bird, who squirmed in protest and was then relieved to feel the tight clutch lessen and be removed.

Rory flew into the air, the flapping of his wings sounding like the sails of a sailing boat being unfurled. He flew high for a few seconds and then soared around the lighthouse, as if seeking confirmation of his flight path from its now automated light. Then he ceased his circling and flew towards home, ignoring the barking of the Labrador that was watching him from the bridge below.

'He'll beat you home,' laughed Hamish.

'He always does, now let's get you home. You've your

Paul to see to.'

'Aye,' replied Hamish as his laugh vanished and seemed

like a distant echo poking fun at his soul.

Alison walked into her kitchen and stood just inside the

doorway. She frowned, she wasn't sure why she had come

into the room.

'Come away in Alison and sit yourself down,'

encouraged Molly. She noticed that her friend was still

wearing yesterday's crumpled clothing. She wondered if

she'd even slept but thought that now was not the time to

ask. She poured from the recently filled teapot. 'Here, you

sip on this,' she said, handing Alison a mug. 'I'm going to

make you a bacon roll. I know that you won't feel like

eating, but I want you to eat it all the same. You need the

strength to get you through this day. And that's what you

do, you take each day as it comes. And accept the help from me and your sisters, that's what friends and family are for.' She nodded and was pleased to see her pal nod back, almost like an automaton in a car factory. She then moved to the cooker and left Alison to her thoughts, which were of Paul, he would never be far from her mind.

'You go in the shower and I'll rustle us up something to eat. I think my parents have had to go to their work,' said Irvine as he looked out of the window and saw that their cars had gone. 'I've told my boss that I won't be in again, I've you to look after.'

Bella nodded. She'd awoken with a start and was distraught at finding that it hadn't all been a bad dream. Her Paul had really gone. She wiped the tears from her face, resolved to try and face this new day without breaking down. Fresh tears smarted her eyes and she knew that she'd be unsuccessful in this promise.

Hamish stood on his doorstep and waved his friend off and then spied a well-polished car pull over across the street. It was a black 4x4, well equipped to reach the remotest rural Aberdeenshire farmhouses during the iciest of weather. A smartly dressed woman, in a two-piece skirt and jacket combination, came out of the car. She carried a thick black case with her, like an old-fashioned carpet bag, though this was of battered leather. It looked like it had been passed down from a father, or other family member. It seemed heavy, despite its compact size. She looked across to Hamish and smiled grimly. The smile was not returned. He gave a brief absent nod of the head and turned around to go back into his home, without another thought about her. As she crossed the road towards him, she called out, 'Don't go in Mr Dewart.'

Hamish turned back and looked across and frowned. He tried to place the woman in his memory and had to dig deep, for he seldom went to the surgery. 'How are you doctor?' he politely asked, though he was puzzled as to why she was here, for he hadn't called the GPs surgery. Perhaps Alison had whilst he'd been out. 'I'm sorry, I hadn't recognised you, it's been a while since I last saw you. I'm fighting fit now.' He frowned, 'Or at least I was until yesterday morning.'

The doctor interrupted his morose thoughts, reached out and placed her free hand by his elbow and gave his arm a soft, gentle, encouraging squeeze and said quietly, 'We're all so sorry to hear about your loss. May I come in please?'

'But of course,' replied Hamish as he opened the door, 'please excuse me forgetting my manners. Did Alison call you?' he asked, still puzzled.

The doctor entered and waited until Hamish had closed the outside door. 'No. One of us comes out whenever a family have lost someone. We've seen that folk often don't look after their own health, so we pop along and see if we can do anything and do a quick informal health check whilst we are here. Is your wife upstairs?'

'No, I'm just here,' said Alison as she walked into their lobby. 'Would you like a cup of tea?'

'No, no, don't you worry about me. Shall we pop into the lounge?' Without waiting for a reply, she opened the lounge door and stood there, marshalling them both inside. They obediently shuffled in and then she closed its glass door. 'I'm so sorry to hear about Paul. One of your pals told me during her appointment first thing this morning.

So, I've come to see how you both are and to see what the surgery can do to help.' She left the question hanging in the air, for the couple to reply and seek whatever help they needed.

'That's really kind doctor,' replied Hamish, taking the initiative as he saw how overcome his wife was by this unexpected kindness. He ushered the doctor to sit down on their sofa.

She briskly walked over and sat down whilst placing onto the carpet her black medical bag with practised ease. 'I shan't ask how you both are, because that would be a daft question, so please let me say that you can call the surgery over the next few weeks and you both, and Bella, will be given a priority appointment and it'll be on the same day. And please don't hesitate to call, we are prepared to stay behind when the surgery officially closes and be there for you.'

Hamish and Alison looked to each other and then to the doctor, overwhelmed by her compassion. 'That's so kind of you doctor,' replied Hamish, 'I hadn't realised that you do that, especially as we know how busy you are and the long hours you work.'

The doctor looked embarrassed and replied, 'No, think nothing of it. We've learned that bereaved folk often neglect their own health,' she repeated. She looked knowingly at Hamish, 'May I talk freely with you both, or would you prefer to speak on your own with me?'

'Don't worry doctor, Hamish and I don't keep anything from each other, we're a bit too long in the tooth to have secrets. I know all about Hamish's anxiety and depression and he knows all my medical ins and outs,' confided Alison. Hamish nodded in silent agreement.

The doctor looked relieved and bent down to her bag and pulled out a box of drugs. 'These are for you Hamish. I strongly advise you to restart your Pregabalin. I know from refreshing my memory from your notes that you'd worked so hard with your mindfulness and had come off the anxiety drugs, but I think that your loss is far too immense for you to cope with alone.'

Hamish nodded. 'My friend Douglas had just left as you arrived. Before he left, he convinced me that I need to take whatever help I get offered and to look after myself. He lost his wife to cancer and lost his way for a while. He worried that it affected his son and was worried the same thing might happen to me and those around me. So, for the sake of Bella and Alison, I'll gladly take them.' He reached forward and took the offered drugs.

'Yes, he sounds a sensible friend. I've given you a few weeks supply of 25mg capsules and would suggest starting at one a night. I've taken the precaution of adding them to your repeat prescription so that you can resupply easily.

Their sedative effect may help you get some sleep too,' she replied, watching for a nod from Hamish before relinquishing her grip on the box. 'I've also slipped in an appointment card for me to see you both as a double appointment, either together or separately one after the other. When you are able, perhaps you can pop the date and time in your diary or calendar, and if it clashes with another commitment, then please call and reschedule it. I anticipate that you'll need to slowly increase to 50mg or 100mg as the weeks progress. That'll minimise any side-effects, and please don't drink alcohol at any time whilst taking them.'

Hamish nodded, thinking back to his dram of whisky in the early hours of yesterday, it was probably the reason he had been able to get to sleep.

'You might find that your nightmares from your army days may return. I'm hoping that by going back on your

Pregabalin they may be minimised. You've enough trauma to be dealing with.'

Alison nodded, what Hamish had to do in the burnt-out truck in Belize was indeed trauma enough. He'd told her little of the incident, but the few scraps of information and memories that he'd shared over the years went a little way to explaining his thrashing nightmares, over this and other incidents.

The doctor, seeing Alison's nodding, turned her attention to her. 'Paul was such a lovely boy, though I've only been in the area for half of my working life, I do remember him as a young teenager. He was always so polite and happy, on the few occasions I saw him at the surgery. He kept in great health. Please acknowledge the huge loss you've both experienced and accept these,' she said passing Alison a small bottle of pills. This time she passed the drugs without hesitation or conditions. 'They are 10mg strength Temazepam, to help you on the nights you can't sleep, or are deeply troubled. This short, one off supply, won't cause any worries about dependency. I'd suggest one tablet a night as needed and if you are still awake by one o'clock you could take another one if you don't need to be awake by 9 o'clock.' She looked to Hamish and then back to Alison, 'but please do watch for any daytime drowsiness on both the pills you are taking, especially if,' she hesitated, aware of how insensitive what she was about to say would sound.

'It's alright doctor, we are both nurses and know what you mean. We should be careful when driving,' stated Hamish as he looked up to his son's photo. He smiled briefly, despite the day. He did love his cheeky wee son.

'Yes, thank you Hamish. Is there anything else I can do for you both, or for Bella?' She looked up to the ceiling, as if able to see through the plasterboard and floorboards. 'Is she still asleep?'

'No, I don't think so,' replied Alison, looking to Hamish. She was relieved that the doctor had dictated to Hamish that he restart his medicines. She was pleased to see him putting the tablets by his drink's coaster, for later in the evening. 'Bella is with her fiancé, but perhaps you could see that she gets an appointment with you, she'd appreciate seeing you on her own.'

The doctor smiled and slipped across an appointment card, 'Our receptionist is very thorough. It's early days yet, but in a few weeks, you might want to make an appointment with the surgery's counsellor. We usually offer four free forty-five-minute sessions, but when I see her at the surgery's next meeting, I'll ask her to extend this. I'd advise seeing her individually. It'll be better for her and I think for you all. You'll have different things to talk about.'

'Yes, that sounds sensible doctor,' acknowledged Hamish. He looked across to the glass door and smiled. He stood up and walked towards it and said, 'Please don't say no, she doesn't acknowledge that word.' He opened the lounge door and missed the puzzled look on the doctor's face.

As the door opened Molly came in with a tray of cups, saucers, a teapot, a small jug of milk, a bowl of sugar and some biscuits. 'I wasn't sure when I should bring this in, so I waited by the door, it's awful heavy for me though,' she blustered as she found herself embarrassed at being caught out, standing by the door.

Hamish acknowledged the hint and took the tray from her, 'Come away in Molly, the doctor was just giving us some pills and advice.' He walked over to the coffee table

285

by the doctor's feet and lowered the goodies-laden tray onto its glass top.

Molly smiled at her, 'Ah! It's yourself lass, oh, you were awfully good to my Bill.'

The doctor smiled, her face reddening at this unexpected praise, 'Ah, yes, how are you?' her question not giving away the fact that she couldn't remember Molly's surname.

'Oh, don't you worry about me, you look after these two. Do you remember how well they helped you look after my Bill? A tower of strength they were. You'll have a cup of tea before you disappear?'

The doctor looked across to Hamish who was vigorously nodding his head.

'That would be lovely, thank you.' She knew that this old lady's name would come to her soon, though the moment to address her had easily passed unnoticed.

'I'll just pour this and be on my way out. I've my washing to attend to and these two are well fed now,' replied Molly as she expertly poured the tea and passed it onto the doctor, along with an offering of various biscuits. The doctor put down her cup and saucer and then her eyes lit up as she spied a Tunnock's teacake and added it to her offered plate. 'Thank you.'

Molly smiled at her, 'I'll be on my way and leave you to look after these two.' She looked across to her neighbours, 'And best you two let someone else do the caring for once. You listen to the doctor's advice. I'll be next door if you need me.' She exited the lounge, off to do her washing, giving her charges no time to argue.

Hamish passed his wife a cup and saucer and said, 'We've found it best to always obey Molly! So please take the opportunity to have a cup of tea and biscuit if you have the time.'

The doctor looked longingly at the treats before her and was already mentally unwrapping the inviting silver and red foil wrapper of the chocolate, marshmallow and biscuit goodie on her plate. She made a conscious decision not to look at the clock on the mantlepiece as she reached for her plate, whilst casually glancing at the other biscuits and cakes on the tray. She knew the other doctors would cover for her and wouldn't be expecting her back at the surgery so quickly. Her stomach rumbled in reminder that she had skipped breakfast this morning to have time to take her daughter to nursery. 'I've all the time you need me for, Alison and Hamish, is there anything else I can do for you?' she casually asked as she slowly unwrapped her chocolate teacake, trying not to let the metallic rustle intrude on this delicate time. 'Have you been able to see Paul yet?'

'No,' little-white-lied Hamish, 'well, only at the police mortuary. You know, to identify him. He should now be at the undertaker's and he thought it best that we see him at about ten o'clock. So, we are waiting for Bella to come home, before going together.'

The doctor nodded, mouth too full to talk as she munched down on the biscuit base, she'd already nibbled at the outer chocolate and squeezed at the delightful marshmallow.

'The police are still doing their investigations, but the forensics team did an early post-mortem and the Procurator Fiscal released his body fine and early. We hope to be able to spend some time with Paul when the undertaker has done what he needs to do.' Hamish looked across to his wife, who had reached into her pullover sleeve for a tissue. He quickly decided not to go to comfort her or make a fuss, he knew that's what she'd prefer just now. He hesitated but decided that the doctor needed to know. 'Paul either wasn't wearing his seatbelt or his airbag failed to go off. He was rear shunted by a drunk driver.'

'Oh!' exclaimed the doctor, putting down her plate and empty wrapper onto the glass table. 'Oh gosh. I'm so sorry. I don't know what to say. But I'm guessing that it would have been quick. He wouldn't have suffered?' she found herself automatically saying, despite not knowing the full facts.

'That's what the police liaison officer said,' interjected Alison, before wiping her tears and blowing her nose.

'There is little comfort in these events, but Paul wouldn't have been in much pain for long?' said the doctor as she reached for her cup and saucer.

'No, I know what you mean,' replied Hamish, 'it's just so awful and I feel so helpless, we both do,' he failed to tell her that he'd rushed to the scene with his medical kit. Not through embarrassment, but because he didn't want to hold up the doctor, he knew she'd have a busy surgery ahead of her. He watched as she sipped at her tea. She'd mastered the art of not looking flustered and of giving the impression that she was there for them both. This was an art that no amount of medical or nursing training could teach you, experience was the educator.

She put down her half-empty cup and replaced the laden saucer to the table. 'Please do call if we can be of help and do take the medicines. This is a catastrophic time for you all and you must take the help you all need. Please let Bella know that she can have an appointment today if she needs it.' She looked up at Paul's photo as she stood up and lifted her bag. 'Such a handsome young man, I'm so sorry that he has left you.' She walked over to the couple who were seated in their armchairs and reached out to pat Alison's shoulder twice whilst expertly holding her black case behind her so that it didn't bang into Alison's knees.

She then quickly walked over to Hamish and reached for his hand to shake. 'Please don't get up, I'll see myself out.' She paused as she reflected and then said, 'Please thank Mrs Ross for my treats.'

Irvine pushed the plate towards Bella. 'Mum won't forgive me if you don't eat them,' he cajoled as he unscrewed the cap for the maple syrup.

Bella looked down at the thick Scottish pancakes, normally these stodgy breakfast treats, known as dropped scones, were her favourite, but her appetite hadn't returned, despite her growling stomach. She reluctantly picked up her knife and fork.

Pleased, Irvine poured a small amount over the top of the pile of pancakes until Bella nodded for him to stop. He replaced the cap and placed the bottle on the table, next to the jar, strawberry jam was his preferred topping. He picked it up, popped its lid open and used his knife to scrape out a liberal amount. He wanted to have a full stomach before seeing his pal later. He knew that it would be respectful to allow Bella and his parents to see Paul as a family and was pleased that Bella had invited him along with them, but his mum had chatted to him earlier and advised him to drop her off at her parents and then arrange to view him later. He picked up his fork and with a look across to Bella to check that she was eating, he dived into his breakfast treat, and, despite the forthcoming event, he ate with relish.

Chapter 16

Irvine glanced at his side and rear-view mirrors as he reversed carefully into his fiancée's driveway. The street was empty of cars, their owners had driven to work, leaving the road barren except for the small blue pensioner's car, several houses away. Irvine was momentarily distracted by the fluttered movement of the net curtain from the adjoining house. 'Molly is watching us,' he said to Bella, breaking the silence of the journey from the adjacent village.

'Oh, she's harmless enough. I expect she's only looking out for mum and dad. She's a lovely old lady really.' She turned around in her seat and gave Molly a cheery wave, though her heart was not in it.

Molly waved back, placed her free hand to her heart and appeared to give it a small thump.

Bella, knowing that she meant she was sending her love, nodded, and seeing that Irvine had finished his parking, gave her the thumbs up sign for her heart wouldn't be in Molly's view. She turned to face her future husband. 'Thank you for looking after me so well, and your mum.' She laughed, 'and your dad, in his own way.'

Irvine returned the laugh, though his was more from nerves. 'Och, that's okay, we are family now. But I'll leave you with yours for some privacy. I don't want to intrude, but I'd like to see Paul, later today.'

'You aren't intruding love, you are family. But yes, I'll have to think of mum and dad and see to them first. I hope you don't mind?'

'Not at all, I don't mind, though you know I'm only a phone call away,' he said as he nodded to his mobile that was cradled in the space by the cigarette lighter, where it was on charge.

'Yes, thank you.' She leant over and kissed him on the cheek.

Irvine turned, so that he could kiss her on the lips, though he wondered if that would be appropriate in the circumstances. Movement in the rear-view mirror caught his eyes and halted his intended action. 'Your folks are on the doorstep, let me see you off and I'll say hello to them.'

Bella nodded her consent and they both exited the car. She looked over to the attached house. Molly was no longer keeping vigil at the window. She walked up to the steps and put out her arms to cuddle her parents. They drew in close and embraced their daughter together. 'Oh, mum and dad,' she cried as she felt their hug get tighter.

Irvine, who had followed Bella from the car and up the steps, looked down at his feet and shuffled nervously from foot to foot. The cold embraced him as he stood there in his shirt and trousers and enveloped him in its iciness like a spectre wrapping a shroud around a cold corpse, readying it for its final journey. He shivered involuntary.

Seeing Irvine shake, Alison broke off her embrace and went to him and gave him a cuddle, as if unconsciously trying to warm him back up. 'Thanks for looking after our girl love,' she sighed. 'You and your parents have been brilliant.' She lowered her voice, 'She'll need lots of looking after in the coming weeks,' she whispered as she broke off the embrace.

Irvine stood straight, as if to face up to the challenge ahead. All thoughts of the cold winter day had been forgotten, thanks to the warming embrace. 'Don't you worry, I'll see that she's okay, but I think you'll want some time alone, to see Paul together.'

Alison nodded, 'Thanks for being understanding. It'll be a hard duty and you don't want to be around as we talk things over with the undertaker and arrange Paul's funeral.'

Irvine nodded reluctantly, he hadn't the heart to tell her that he so wanted that. He wanted to get involved in giving his pal the best send-off any mate could have. Instead he helpfully said, 'I'll go around all his chums and break the news to those who haven't already heard,' he said, trying hard not to point to his phone in the car. He knew that Paul's friends on Facebook would already be messaging each other to break the news. No doubt his wall on his profile page would be full of condolences. Irvine had thought long and hard last night in-between spells of consoling Bella. He'd made his mind up to arrange for a football shaped wreath in the colours of his beloved Aberdeen team. It'd be from all the mates he'd worked with, those from school and all the clubs he'd been a member of as a child. He'd continued many of these friendships into adulthood. Irvine would ask them all to chip in so that the family would know he was loved and respected. He felt a firm hand on his shoulder and broke off his reverie.

'Thanks for looking after Bella, so… er, Irvine,' stuttered Hamish, now tongue-tied at trying to get the word son out. He looked down at his shoes, as if embarrassed at not being able to call his soon to be son-in-law by the affectionate title son. 'Aye, well,' he continued to stutter as he looked up to Irvine. 'Thank you, son,' he finally and determinately said.

Irvine looked up at him proudly. 'That's what family do, dad,' he simply stated.

Molly reluctantly piled the washing into her tumble drier. There was still a dreich feel to the air, and she knew that she'd be wasting her time hanging out her washing today, it'd probably come back in even damper. Besides it felt disrespectful to be getting on with domestic life when next door was hung with grief. They hadn't even opened their blinds yet, and she knew that their sorrow would be shown for all the neighbourhood to see by them not being opened for at least a week, and perhaps not even until after the funeral was held. When her Bill passed on, she hadn't opened hers for a fortnight. She wanted to shut the outside world out. It was Alison who had discreetly opened them one day over coffee. It was her way of saying that life must, however reluctantly, go on. Thereafter, Molly had slowly built a life without her Bill, with the help of her dear neighbours. She turned on the machine and it gave its faint hum like a small propeller-driven aircraft happily flying over an ocean.

Happy with the settings, she then moved over to her cupboards, doing a stock-check of the biscuits and cakes needed to supplement the box that Isaac had delivered. She didn't want to dig too deeply into his generosity and would use her reserves for the days ahead. Satisfied with her counting, she then hummed a song as she walked through to her lounge to watch her favourite Victoria Derbyshire programme on the television. She'd missed the beginning but would soon catch up.

Irvine's fingers hesitated on the horn button of his steering wheel. No, it would be inappropriate to give a cheery toot goodbye. He knew that he'd said a respectful goodbye to his future parents-in-law and his Bella and would leave it at that. He indicated, looked around him and in the mirrors and turned right. As he straightened up into the main road, he felt forward and switched on the radio. Music hadn't felt appropriate in his earlier journey and he now needed something to fill the silence. Happy by

Pharrell Williams belted out of his speakers. It felt incongruous to the mood that he felt himself in, but then he heard the lyrics a bit clearer as the words *happy, happy, happy*, were repeated by the singer. It kind of summed up his best pal's philosophy of life and soon he found himself singing away as he drove to the florist to get an estimate of the cost of a very special wreath.

Hamish toyed with his car key absently, allowing the ring of the keychain to fall in and out of his fingers. He then fretted at the legs of the Lego figurine that was attached to the cord. It was Batman, a present from Paul's visit to Legoland in Windsor. Whenever he'd needed a rare lift in his father's old car, he'd joke, 'To the Batmobile!' at the same time as his father unhooked the key from the row of keys hanging in the kitchen. Now Hamish would give anything to hear his son's voice belt out those fun-filled words. He'd wonder if he'd ever forget how his son sounded, just like he'd soon forgotten his nana's voice. No matter, it was the emotion behind the voices that mattered. The love would never fade, and that was all that mattered.

'You okay dad?' asked a worried Bella.

Hamish broke from his dreaming and smiled forlornly at his beautiful daughter, the best of Alison and him. 'Aye lass, I was just thinking of our Paul. He may have left us, but his spirit lives on in us. The precious memories of all the good times we had.'

Bella smiled, saw her dad continue to fret at the Lego figurine and his keys and reached over and clasped his face in her hands. 'He loved you, as do I. You're a great dad.'

Alison looked on with tears in her eyes as she watched her husband struggle with his own tears, trying to be brave for his daughter. She was touched to see him stop his nervous movements and reach up and clasp his daughter's hands. He kept them there for a few seconds and then gently removed them and guided them to his lips. He tenderly kissed them and then looked her in the eyes and said, 'I love you too lass.' Their hand-holding broke off a few seconds later and Hamish appeared to steel himself before saying, 'Let's see if we can see our Paul yet. I want you both to have the type of funeral that you want for our boy, then we have to think about what his friends would like too, we mustn't forget them.'

Each nodded their agreement and the broken family made their way to their car, though one seat would always be empty.

A passing grey cloud threatened to drop rain upon the huge expanse of the brick lock-blocked parking area. Its colour and vast shape dominated the skyline, projecting its hue onto the mood of the occupants of the car that sat outside the single-storied funeral home. The front rooms of the building had their blinds discreetly drawn, for these were the resting rooms where souls waited for their mourners to pay their last respects. To the left was another parking area and two large double garages where hearses could be unobtrusively reversed to load or unload their cargo of empty spirit husks. A larger building, set back within the grassed area and annexed, was the Celebration Hall, where humanist services of thanksgiving could be held. The undertaker had thought of everything when he'd had these premises purpose built. Hamish surveyed the one shop service for the families of the dead and cynically thought it to be a great cash cow for the undertaker's deep pockets. Though he also knew how hard he would have worked for his profit. He gripped the steering wheel harder, as if to help summon up energy and to dispel his anger that still raged within him for the drunk driver that had ended his son's life.

Alison reached across and took his left hand from the steering wheel and rested both their hands on his lap, 'Shall we go in, before the rain starts and soaks us?'

'Will we be able to hold Paul's hand?' asked Bella quietly from the backseat.

'Aye lass, we'll be able to see him together. Let's go in and see our Paul,' replied Hamish as he reluctantly let go of his wife's hand. *'I never thought I'd see the day where I had to arrange the funeral for my own son,'* he despondently thought as he exited the car. He looked up at the murky clouds hanging above him like a dark cape waiting to engulf him in self-pity. He compared them to the deeply unsettling thoughts that he was having. Taking the Pregabalin was the right advice by the doctor, he knew that it would soon stop his mind spiralling deeper into a dark pit of despair. He knew from bitter experience that it was hard to dig yourself out from that bottomless trench of hopelessness once you find yourself in it. He looked across and saw that his wife and daughter were out of the car and then he locked it. He toyed absently with his Batman Lego figurine and would have given his soul away to the devil just for one more minute of having his son back, and as a youngster and content to be building a made-up space ship from the odds and ends of his bricks, bought during their family visit to Legoland in Windsor. If only he could give his life away and have his son alive once more, but it doesn't work like that. He sighed and walked to the entrance, the clouds seemed to follow him, shutting out the light as he shuffled along, as if to mock his dark mood and show him that his life was darkness from now on. He ignored the doorbell and tried the door. It opened. He expected a creak like in a cheap and cliched horror film, but it opened silently. He moved back with the door, allowing Alison and Bella to enter, though he did wonder whether he should enter first, to ensure all was well, or whether he should be chivalrous. But he knew these stupid thoughts were just that, his mood was making him hyper-vigilant again and he fought against his instincts and deeply-ingrained army training and experience. All was safe here, though he felt emotionally in turmoil.

They waited in the reception area, and all three sat down around a coffee table that was free of magazines, after all, who read at an Undertakers? Though that hadn't stopped the business-headed funeral director from adding a few leaflets about pre-paid funerals to save the heartache of loved ones the expense and difficult decisions. It was such a con, though it was well marketed, tugging at the heartstrings when folk were most emotionally vulnerable, he thought. Though Alison and Hamish had already left instructions in their will with the family solicitor that they'd like to be buried in the local cemetery and that they'd like their Nursing Corps cap-badges engraved on their headstones. It seemed fitting as they'd met in the Corps and two members had delivered their children. It had been a big part of their lives that they'd been proud of, though their children had made them prouder. Hamish reached over to his wife and daughter and took hold of their hands and gave each a gentle squeeze that silently spoke volumes of his love. He let go as he heard soft footsteps upon the carpeted hallway.

A hacking cough bounced along the walls and floor interrupting the sombre quietness of the funeral parlour. The noise seemed to settle high, upon the ceiling and dissipate out along the paintwork, before settling out onto a diminishing echo. This was followed by a distinct wheeze as the undertaker struggled to catch his breath.

Hamish wondered what exertions had caused this difficulty in his breathing and if it was turning and washing his son. He'd wondered about asking if he could perform this last act for his child. Mr Green rounded the corner, and Hamish, recognising the old man as the undertaker, from news stories in the local paper, over the years, could see that he had his white shirt sleeves rolled up and had been doing something messy. The low cut of his black waistcoat did not reveal any stains and Hamish pondered upon what chemicals he'd be filling Paul with. Perhaps it was best he didn't know and just left the expert to it. He had to take a step back and allow others to take on the caring role. Everything just seemed so unnatural to him. He held out his hand in greeting. 'Hello, Mr Green I presume, I'm Hamish and this is Alison, my wife, and this is Bella, our daughter.'

Mr Green took the offered hand, 'Please call me Brendan,' he replied as he pumped Hamish's hand.

Hamish looked down at the long-spindly fingers that were intertwined with his. They would be undressing, washing, embalming and dressing his son. He imagined them spider-like, crawling and feeling around Paul, being intimate in a way that should only be the right of a parent. He so wanted to wash away the blood-stains from his son and soothe his scratches and wounds with some restorative balm. Instead, he returned the firm, strong handshake that was incongruous to the wraith-like appearance this thin man projected. 'Thank you, Brendan, for looking after our Paul so quickly.' He looked to Bella and Alison who were both nodding slowly in silent agreement.

Brendan relieved himself from the handshake and quickly shook hands with Alison and Bella. 'I'm so sorry that we have to meet in these circumstances, please follow me to a quieter room where we won't be disturbed.' He led the way down a corridor, opposite to the one he had come from. '*The parlour complex was spider-legged like too,*' thought Hamish grimly. '*And how much quieter does he need it to be?*' he morosely thought as he passed rooms numbered one through to seven, like in a nursing home, though in these bedrooms the patients slept eternally. He absently wondered what room number would be allocated to Paul, or if indeed his son was already in one of the rooms. The stillness of the building settled upon the grieving trio without their knowledge or consent and weighed heavily upon their frames, pushing down and burdening them further as they obediently followed the undertaker. Hamish allowed himself to be told and led. It felt so alien to him, but he resigned himself, albeit reluctantly, to the care of this professional.

Brendan opened the door at the end of the dimly lit corridor and entered a bright room, tastefully painted in yellow pastels broken up by a thin border of orange swirled wallpaper that was hung around the centre of the walls. There were several comfortable looking chairs and he pointed over to them and beckoned the trio in with his thin, stretched, fingers, as if he was the skeletal ferryman Charon in Hades motioning for his passengers to enter his boat so that they could cross the Styx and Acheron rivers. Hamish willed himself not to shudder at the thought of this stranger's hands upon his wounded Paul's flesh.

The trio sat down, and Hamish couldn't help but notice that more leaflets about paying for your funeral upfront were scattered upon the low table, like tempting holiday brochures at a travel agent. He really was touting this payment plan, though in a discrete way. His thoughts were interrupted by the undertaker's wheezing and again

Hamish found himself thinking that the old boy might not be up to the job. Perhaps he should have used the firm in the next town. It was equally as close to their home and the cemetery. *'I wonder if he needs to take a few puffs on an inhaler,'* he thought, ever the nurse. *'I think he may have chronic obstructive pulmonary disease and may not know it?'* He kept silent, not wanting to upset the man responsible for his son's care, though worrying and feeling guilt at not being able to help another.

'Paul is now in our care, my son's just attending to him now,' rasped Brendan, fighting the urge to cough. Instead, he distractedly splayed his long spindly fingers out, just above his waist, as if getting ready to pray. They rose slightly higher and he interlaced them, trying to settle them onto his pigeon-like chest, instead he opted to continue rubbing them together, almost like he was awaiting payment.

'*Perhaps in his mind he was totting up his bill,*' thought Hamish, distracted by the man's hand-wringing movements.

'Yes,' continued the undertaker, his fingers appearing to writhe and twist at a furious pace now, 'Paul is in our care,' he firmly stated.

Hamish looked relieved and his shoulders visibly sagged as the burden of worry as to the undertaker's fitness to practice was taken from him. A younger, and fitter man was taking care of his Paul. He wondered if he too had the long bony fingers of his father.

'Can we see him,' asked a desperate Alison, the urgency apparent for all to hear.

The undertaker shook his head slowly, 'No, I would strongly advise against it.'

'Oh,' said a shocked Bella, looking at both of her parents with a deeply troubled look as if to say, '*but you both promised.*'

Alison reached over to take Bella's hands in hers. 'Why not?' she demanded of the undertaker. 'He looked okay at the police morgue, his face was relatively unscathed from the accident.'

Brendan shook his head more vigorously as he repeated the word, 'No,' but more authoritatively. 'I'm afraid that there is fresh scarring after his post-mortem, you know, after the pathologist had run her tests.'

'That's odd,' interjected a confused Hamish. 'I've seen some post-mortems carried out, and they leave little scarring for the family to see. They normally have the Y-shaped incision from the shoulders and chest, but surely you would be covering Paul in a shroud. We only need to see his face and hold his hands. Can't you do that for us?'

'No, please do accept my professionalism here. Paul had to undergo extensive testing because of the nature of his death,' replied the undertaker as he thrummed his fingers against a clipboard that he'd picked up from the bookcase as he had entered the room.

Hamish tried to ignore the distracting motion of the undertaker's fingers, though his confused mind was once again comparing them to a spider's legs. With each thrum movement and sound he thought them to be like the slow, tentative movements of an arachnid's limbs moving furtively around a room, unseen by its humans.

The thrumming continued at a faster, more impatient pace. 'I would strongly advise against viewing him, I would insist on a closed casket funeral. His skin has badly broken down.'

Hamish looked across to Alison and her eyes communicated her acknowledgement of what he was thinking. She nodded in encouragement.

'Alison and I were army nurses and saw some awful sights,' explained Hamish. 'Even working in the NHS has given us some things we'd rather not have seen or done. Please don't worry about us fainting. Please let us see our son,' Hamish pleaded. He looked across to his daughter and saw that she was fighting back her tears. 'We can see our Paul first and then decide if Bella and others like her fiancé should see him.'

'No,' said the undertaker adamantly. 'I really must insist. It's for your own good,' he said firmly. He lowered his voice to barely a whisper and ceased his finger drumming, 'You don't want to see your boy like this, remember him as he was, please. Even his hands are too badly damaged to hold.' He looked at each of the family members in turn.

'I've been an undertaker in the town for over forty years. I started as a junior in the old firm in the Valley View Road premises, run by Mr Dobson. I worked my way up to a senior position and when I learned that Mr Dobson was soon to retire without an heir, I took out a huge bank loan and had this purpose-built funeral parlour constructed. I've cared for many of the big families in town and have built up a respected reputation, please believe me that you don't want to see your son like this. I wouldn't like to see my son if he looked like your Paul, even though I too have seen plenty of bodies and had to perform certain tasks through the decades.' He looked around the grieving family, almost in challenge to defy his order.

He met with no resistance, he could see that each of them had drooped their shoulders and had visibly sagged forward in their resignation.

'*I can't believe that I'm getting into a dick-measuring competition with the undertaker,*' thought Hamish. '*He's trying to out-measure Alison and I about the sights we've seen. I only want to see my Paul.*' He broke off these dark thoughts and tried to concentrate his mind to the issue in hand. He put his hand into his pocket and took out his Batman Lego keyring. He then tried to discretely remove it from his bunch of keys.

Alison broke the silence, 'Can we spend some time with him in his closed coffin. I'd like to pray by it please?' she almost begged.

Brendan smiled, 'But of course. There are a few questions I must ask first and there are some forms I need to fill out. Shall I begin, or do you need a moment?' He looked around the room.

Alison looked to her daughter and husband and told Brendan, 'No, we are fine,' she decided.

Brendan smiled, almost triumphantly, as if he had the family firmly in his grip. 'There are some services we offer. Shall I arrange with the local newspaper to put an announcement about Paul's passing and the funeral details?'

'No,' said Hamish, 'We'd like to keep the funeral intimate, just us and his friends.'

'Oh,' said Brendan, 'normally that would be the done thing, the expected thing,' he emphasised. He again looked around the room, as if challenging the family to defy his routine, to cut into his profits.

'No,' firmly stated Hamish. 'There's no need for things like that. Let's just do it how we want it.' He wriggled free the keychain and held it out in the palm of his hand. 'I'd like this to go in the coffin with Paul please. I'd like him to be holding it. It was a gift from him, and I'd like him to know just how much it and he meant to me. I'd also like to put the ashes of our family dog, Captain, and a cuddly toy in the coffin too. It'll be the one that I took on operations. It was handmade by Bella when she was young, with lots of help from Alison. They'd always sneak it into my rucksack, to keep me safe when overseas. It was a..'

He was cut off by the undertaker who replied, 'Yes, I've been an undertaker here for over forty-five years, man and boy. I've built up a great reputation and am trusted by the locals. They always have funeral notices in the paper and they always say that their loved ones are resting here. It's most unusual not to have them,' he appeared to puff out his chest, as if in pride, or perhaps to catch his breath after such a speech.

The family looked at one another, shocked at the impertinence of this man, interrupting Hamish, cutting him short. Alison wondered if it was too late to change undertakers. She was beginning to have her doubts over the competence and caring nature of this man who was entrusted to see Paul laid to rest.

The undertaker carried on, unabashed. He put a large cross beside a tick box in the form he was working through. 'It'll look bad on us,' he muttered under his breath, underlining the cross several times for emphasis. 'No matter.' He then looked through his papers and pulled out a form and handed it to Hamish. 'You'll need to take this to the Registry Office, preferably today. It's to register Paul's death. You'll need his birth certificate. He leaned forward and pointed to a circled telephone number with his index finger, like a harbinger of doom pointing to a condemned man. He circled the number and then gave a few taps onto the paper, as if choosing who would be led to the gallows. He leant back, his pointed finger still aimed at Hamish. It wavered for a few minutes and then returned to rest with the other talon-like digits.

'Thank you,' said Hamish, not knowing that else to say.

'There isn't a great deal else to do, until you've done that. Then I can arrange the funeral, phone the crematorium, unless you'd prefer burial?'

'Yes, we'd like Paul buried, in the village graveyard, we'd like to buy two plots if we can, so that we can be laid to rest beside him, when it's our turn,' said Alison, fighting desperately to hold back the tears.

The undertaker relinquished his hold on his clipboard, with its important notes and his pen. They balanced precariously on his knees for his whole body appeared to shake with a fast movement caused by his hands writhing and twisting like a basket full of snakes. A rictus unpleasant grin appeared momentarily on his face before he halted all movement and briskly picked up his pen and paper once more and started furiously ticking at boxes. 'A church service?' he tentatively enquired.

'We don't really believe in all that, sorry not any more, though I do say a prayer, now and then,' said Alison. 'After all the deaths we've seen, it's hard to believe in a caring, loving God. Though I will be praying for my boy today, you know, old habits.'

The handwringing recommenced as the undertaker nestled his notes on his knees again, 'We can offer the use of our hall and perhaps a Humanist service?' he boldly suggested. 'There is a chap nearby who is so kind and gentle and can come along to your home and learn all about Paul so that he can talk at the funeral?'

'That sounds lovely, doesn't it, mum and dad?' interjected Bella.

The undertaker was nodding furiously at the couple, hoping to project obedience into them.

'Aye, right enough,' said Hamish, 'Though, if I can get my emotions in check, I'd like to say a few words, you know, about Paul's life and all the joy he brought...'

'That's settled then,' interrupted the undertaker again, 'you all just leave it with me, and I'll see to Paul and take good care of him and you all.' He picked up his papers and started ticking boxes with a flourish of his pen. Then he turned over the last sheet on the clipboard. 'Okay, now Paul was a tall lad,' said the undertaker, leaving the question carefully balanced in the air.

It was picked up by Bella as she innocently answered, 'Five foot eleven inches he is, er was,' she hesitantly said as she pulled out a tissue from the box on the table in front of her.

'Ah, but we have to allow for his feet to drop,' said a triumphant Brendan, pleased that the young girl had fallen for his little joke. 'That's why coffins are so long at the bottom.'

Bella began to cry, distressed at the realisation that her brother was truly gone and would soon be all alone in the ground. She reached over to her mother and felt her comforting hands surround her.

'Perhaps not go into such detail please,' whispered Hamish, cross at the way this undertaker was performing his act. 'This is the first death for Bella. There are things she need not know.'

'Perhaps it's time to choose a coffin for,' he hesitated and quickly looked down at his forms, 'for Paul to rest in. There are some lovely walnut and oak coffins that look so much brighter for younger folk to rest in. Mahogany can appear so aging. They also slow down the rot, well you know.'

Hamish sighed, not at the inevitability of it all, but at the crass way Brendan was going about his business. He was regretting using this firm.

Brendan ignored the sigh, mistaking it for a grieving father trying to maintain his composure. 'Paul can then rest on a bed of velvet, come with me and I'll show you several models we have.' He rose to his feet and walked out of the room and down the subtly-lit corridor, leaving the family no option, but to follow obediently.

Chapter 17

The heady scent of the floral displays threatened to engulf Irvine as he breathed in deeply to help concentrate his mind. He felt the hairs in his nostrils fight out against the pollen that overpowered their delicate structure as they twitched in protest to this alien environment.

'Hello, how can I help you,' asked the middle-aged woman whose jeans and pullover were part hidden by her green tabard. She smoothed down this garment as she walked over to the counter, habitually brushing down stray petals.

Irvine committed himself by firmly closing the door to the shop, against the cold and rain shower, feeling that his grief was real now that he was about to buy his best pal a wreath. The jingle of the doorbell above the door was still resounding against the frame and its joviality seemed to be mocking this young mourner. He hesitated in his response and was carelessly looking around this unfamiliar environment.

Sensing his discomfort, the florist finished smoothing down her garment and was now pushing loose hairs back behind her ears. She smiled at the young man before her. The greeting was not returned. Unperturbed, she stepped from the counter and over to the young man and whispered, 'I'm guessing that it's not flowers for a happy occasion?'

Still overcome from the magnitude of what was before him today, Irvine merely shook his head. He did not trust his voice, not fully, it would only betray the depth of his sorrow.

'Is it flowers for a loved one?' she gently enquired.

'Yes, my best friend,' whispered Irvine, relieved that his voice had held. He started edging towards her, committing himself by going further into the shop. In a firmer voice he said, 'He died yesterday, I need to buy a wreath from all his pals, and from me.'

'Oh, I'm so sorry. He must have been so young. What was his name?'

'Paul, he was only twenty-two, he was to be my best man, I should be marrying his sister in a few months.'

'Oh heavens, you poor thing,' sighed the florist. She couldn't help comparing the two occasions, one of deep sorrow, and the other one of extreme happiness that would be tinged with the heartache of one so missed and absent from the happy event. 'May I give you a hug?'

Irvine nodded, still not fully trusting his emotions. He held out his arms and allowed himself to be hugged tight against the rough cloth of the tabard. His nasal hairs twitched at the fresh outbreak of pollen. He broke off the hug as he struggled to contain a sneeze that ejected as soon as the woman was clear. 'I'm so sorry,' he mumbled.

'Oh, bless you,' she instinctively said, almost reverently, like a padre hearing a soldier's confession before a battle.

'I'm sorry, I shouldn't be in here,' exclaimed Irvine.

'It's okay love, you can always come back later, you know, if it's too much.' She pointed through a doorway, 'Or we could go out back, into the patio, if you prefer to sit down. You'll be all alone there, and then you can come back through when you feel up to it.'

Irvine fished out a paper tissue from his jeans pocket from a supply he'd thought to take along. He blew his nose. 'Sorry, you don't understand, I have hay fever. I'm normally alright over the winter months. I usually avoid flower shops. I think my fiancée gets upset that I don't buy her flowers, but you see what happens when I'm near them.' He held the soggy tissue up to his nose and shrugged a further apology.

'Ah, I understand. I'm afraid there's no getting away from them here,' she replied, deliberately not turning the phrase into a joke, she'd tried to keep it matter of fact. This was the part of the job she hated, happy occasions were so much lighter and easier to accommodate, well, except for the bridezillas. Or their mothers, and often both simultaneously. 'Did you want some help in choosing the type of wreath for Paul,' she helpfully suggested.

'I've one in mind. You see he loved Aberdeen Football Club, so I wondered if you could do a wreath, you know, shaped like a football, but with his team colours? Is that possible please?'

'That would be a thoughtful and touching tribute to your friend. Yes, that's easy enough. We could also do one shaped like a football shirt, still with his team colours, then a sash below with his name. Would you prefer that instead?'

'No, I really want a football. It's how we met, playing football at secondary school. He lived in the next village, so I didn't know him at primary school. But we became great mates as teenagers. It'll be from all his pals though. I've set up a crowdfunding page this morning, while his parents and sister visit the undertakers, and a few friends have already donated.'

'That's such a lovely thing to do. His family will be so touched,' she walked back to the counter and reached under it. 'Come over here, away from most of the stronger flowers and have a look at these photos. The starting price is eighty-five pounds and that'll include a card. I'd suggest selecting one of our larger ones, then if any of his pals wants to sign it the day before, or even on the morning of the funeral, they can.'

Irvine walked over, 'I can definitely afford to give you fifty pounds now, I'm afraid that's all I have in my bank account until I'm next paid. But his friends have already donated twenty pounds the last time I looked at the webpage.' He toyed nervously at his jacket pocket, wondering whether to bring his mobile out to prove his providence.

'Don't you worry too much about that. It'll be a day or two before I can make a start. We have a regular order for the flowers, we use a lovely double spray of chrysanthemums. It's a popular choice, but I won't bring some sample flowers over to you. I don't want to set you off snee...'

Her sentence was cut off by another almighty sneeze by Irvine. He quickly blew his nose. 'Thank you, so, er, how much would it be to also have something like, a great friend to all, on a ribbon?'

'That would be a lovely thing for the family to see. Yes, that can be done. We work with a local printer. But that would be part of our deluxe package I'm afraid.' She looked across to him, disappointed that she had to charge such high prices, though she tried to keep her profit margin low for funerals, to help the recently bereaved local families.

'Oh, how much would that be,' asked Irvine as he flicked through the laminated brochure, looking at the pictures and trying hard not to see the prices first.

'It would be one hundred and ten pounds, I'm afraid,' she looked abashed as she continued, 'I'm afraid I can't make it any cheaper, I do try and keep my costs down for funerals,' she tried explaining, faltering at the last words.

'Oh. Just bear with me please,' Irvine said as he unzipped his jacket pocket and pulled out his phone. He flicked through the screens until he found his Just Giving page and involuntarily whistled through his teeth. He looked up to the florist and couldn't help but smile as he said, 'It's already at four hundred pounds!'

'Oh, how lovely, he must have been a popular lad, he's going to be missed.'

'Yes, he is, he was, he will be,' replied Irvine, correcting himself. The smile was now a distant memory, 'but we can show his family that he was loved by many.'

The florist quickly summed up in her head her hours of work for this week and balanced them against her other orders and came to a decision, she could just about do it, if she worked well into the evenings. 'We could add a green area below the football with more flowers and make it look like it is on turf, like on a pitch. Or you could donate the money to whatever charity the family choose for a collection on the day of the funeral. That would also be a great way to remember your pal.'

'I didn't realise there would be a charity collection, I don't know much about funerals I'm afraid. This is my first one,' he said absently, before making up his mind. 'I think we'll stick with the original wreath, the football on its own. We always played on concrete anyway. I think the school sold the fields to a developer years ago. But can we please have the deluxe package?'

The florist smiled warmly and touched Irvine on the shoulder, 'That's a great choice and I'll have the time this week to make that extra special for the same price. I shan't start until Thursday though, so how about you come back then and pay me, you'll have collected the money from your pals by then?' she gently probed.

'Yes, that's no problem,' he looked to his phone and noticed that the page had automatically refreshed itself. The balance now stood at five hundred pounds as word had spread. 'I can transfer the money from the account into my bank account and then pay you in cash. I'll see you then.' He smiled, stifled a sneeze and walked off, wondering where the nearest chemist was.

'Hello, hello,' yelled out the undertaker as he marched the family down a dimly lit corridor. 'I'm walking through with the Dewart family. We are going to be looking at the coffins and furniture. Do you need to close doors?'

Hamish sighed again at the insensitivity of the man. Perhaps his decades in this business had made him impervious to just how indelicate his routines were. He kept abreast with him though, whilst Bella was a few steps behind, being comforted by Alison. He looked to the open doorway that was a few strides away and could see what looked like drab kitchen cabinets. Upon the marble tops were various jars, solutions, swabs and a machine that looked like an old-fashioned suction machine from a hospital. But what caught Hamish's eyes were the feet on the ceramic table. He knew this would be the embalming room. The feet were bluey-grey, but intact. No scratches or cuts disfigured them. They were wrinkle free and there was no sagging skin, they looked like a young man's feet. He so wanted to rush into the room and see if that was his Paul. This was his opportunity to hold his son, to cradle him and whisper '*I love you,*' into his ear as he stroked his face. The age and size of the feet would be about right. The urge to burst into the room was so strong and almost overpowering, he mentally fought against his instincts. Just as he was weighing up whether to break with decorum and go into an uninvited room, the decision was made for him. From within, a large male hand, with fat hairy fingers gripped the door tight, as if weighing up in which direction to slam it. Dirt was buried deep within its nails, incongruous to the clinical cleanliness that made the room so sterile-looking. Then, decision made, it released its grip and, surprisingly gently for such a clumsy-looking hand, it pushed the door closed with a soft click. Silence emanated from the room, almost challenging Hamish to enter at his peril.

'Just through here, if you please,' said Brendan, breaking into the void of Hamish's thoughts as the chasm between man and son widened and mocked his inner being.

Hamish felt sick and struggled to contain his stomach contents, a sudden light-headedness threatened to overwhelm him. He fought against it and continued to walk as directed. Molly and Douglas had been so kind and full of empathy, and now he was experiencing soulless business from a man who should know better, and he was paying, heavily, for the privilege. But he felt compelled to go through with the charade, for the sake of his family. He entered the room, with his family behind him.

They came to a staggering halt, like new recruits learning drill on the parade square, almost comically bumping into each other at the *'squad halt'* command. The sudden realisation of burying their son and brother hit them like a slap to the face as they looked upon the deep room and saw rows upon rows of coffins. Most were closed, and a few were seductively open to display their silken velvety inners, like a macabre brothel. The colours of the coffins ranged from light teak through to sombre deep mahogany.

'Oh my...' declared Bella, 'Our Paul's gone, isn't he?' She left the question in the air, knowing the answer, but wanting to seek confirmation from her parents, like a confused toddler being dropped off at nursery for the first time.

'Yes love, he is,' sighed Hamish as he drew her to him. 'I'm afraid so. Would you like to choose his coffin, he'd like that, he knows that you had good taste and...'?

'And the furniture, love,' interrupted Brendan, wheezing from the exertion of the brief walk. His fingers crept out and found a doorframe to rest against. His digits settled upon the wood, almost skeletal like.

'Furniture?' replied a puzzled Bella, looking at her father, ignoring the undertaker. 'You mean the seats we sit on next to his coffin?'

Brendan emitted a laugh that broke into a coughing, rattling fit. His grin broke, displaying his nicotine-stained teeth, as he pursed his lips to try and gather more air into his damaged lungs. He held up his arm, almost to the stop gesture, as if to belay any help from the family. None was given. Each was growing more resentful to his mannerisms and lack of bedside manner.

'He means the handles and screws Bella,' whispered Hamish. 'Traditional undertakers call those fittings the furniture. We'll be finished soon, and then we can get a coffee somewhere, or go home, whatever you prefer,' he comfortingly said.

'I'd like to go and see Irvine, if you both don't mind?' she looked to both of her parents.

They nodded their heads in unison, 'You be with him love,' Alison insisted, 'we can go to the registrar and do all the necessary things.'

'Yes, so here is our range of coffins, I'd particularly suggest a lighter wood, it'll be more in fitting with the youthfulness of your son.'

For once, Hamish found himself agreeing with Brendan as he walked over to the coffin the undertaker was pointing too. He absently ran his fingers over the wood, following a pattern of the timber, circling his fingers around its route. He felt the warmth of his wife's fingers on his and ceased his preoccupied wanderings. 'Something nice and comfortable for the lining, I know it sounds daft, because he won't feel it, but I want our son to be comfortable.'

Alison and Bella nodded their agreement, they did not think it strange.

Hamish looked across to the undertaker who was wringing his hands, as if trying to wash blood from his fingers. He thought back to Belize and shuddered.

'Sorry, we keep it cold in here, it's better for when we apply the varnish. We like to make our own coffins here you see. Though we buy in the furniture,' said the undertaker, mistaking Hamish's shudder for a shiver. He continued his handwringing in rhythmic timing, almost like he was turning each rotation to the cost of the coffin and fittings, using his turning digits like a bodily calculator.

Hamish watched in almost growing contempt as the handwringing failed to stop, it was almost frenzy-like, perhaps a compulsion. He looked away, back to the open

coffin, imagining his son there. He needed to see him and

hold him. Yet he had to trust this man to have made the

correct decision for his family. But a father's need

overwhelmed his emotions and logic and he looked to the

furniture in more detail, as if choosing, though his mind

was calculating, though far more paternally and less

monetarily than the undertaker.

Irvine's car pulled up to the undertakers, two spaces away

from his future father-in law's vehicle and after he'd

applied his handbrake, he turned off the radio. It didn't

seem right to be listening to music within this solemn area.

After buying antihistamine tablets and a drink, his instincts

had told him to come here. He switched off the engine and

looked down to the ground, the greyness of the lock-block

bricked parking area matched his mood. He then looked

over to the shuttered windows of the foreboding building and wondered if his pal was within. He deliberated over what state his body would be in and whether he'd be brave enough to view him, either alone or with Bella. He certainly didn't want her seeing his dread. He bit his lip to stop himself from crying. He wanted to be brave for Bella. He looked over and saw the bereaved family, his bereaved family, walk out of the undertakers and towards their car. He gave it a respectful few seconds before getting out of his car.

Bella broke free from her mother's hand, like an errant toddler spying a swing, and ran over to be with her fiancé. He held out his arms and allowed her to run into them and almost collapse. He could feel her weight as he forced her upright and held her tight. They remained coupled for several minutes, no words needed. Finally, she broke her silence and declared, 'Oh Irvine, what are we going to do without Paul. He's really dead, he's inside there, all alone and we can't be with him.'

'Did you not get to see him?' he gently asked, stroking her hair, once more wondering if this action was to comfort her, or him.

She shook her head. Not to free herself from his soothing strokes, but in answer to his question. 'It's so unfair, mum and dad promised that I'd get a chance to hold his hand, but that undertaker won't let us see him. It must be a closed coffin viewing. We can sit in a room with him later, but we can't see him or hold him.' She burst into fresh tears again and buried her head into Irvine's shoulders, as if to escape from this waking nightmare.

Irvine's shoulders sagged, not from the weight of Bella's head, but from the relief that he'd not be made to look and spend time with a disfigured corpse, even though it was his best friend. 'Oh Bella,' was all he could bring himself to say.

Bella continued crying, and between bouts of recovery she whispered, 'It's so unfair,' and then fresh cascades of sobbing reignited themselves.

Hamish walked over to his daughter, impotent at not being able to help her. He raised his arms, as if to embrace her, but then he hung back, unsure as to how to make this better for her. He merely nodded to Irvine, a gesture of encouragement and an acknowledgement that his paternal duty was done, now it was up to her future husband to be her strength. 'I'm sorry love,' he softly whispered. It was carried in the wind that gently breezed past, like a fairy gliding through a forest. And like this unseen sprite, it was ignored by unbelievers.

Bella broke off suddenly from Irvine's embrace. She quickly turned to her father and swiftly raised her arm. The finger was pointing straight at him, like a dagger in an assailant's hand. 'BUT YOU PROMISED!' she shouted at him, spittle flying from her mouth. She ignored it and it was soon joined by tears which mingled on the ground. 'YOU PROMISED THAT I COULD HOLD PAUL'S HAND. YOU PROMISED ME!'

'Oh love, I know I did, but the undertak…'

'NO! You made me a promise,' repeated Bella, like a cult mantra.

'But it was out of my hands love, you must see that,' begged Hamish, stepping forward to comfort his daughter.

Her finger remained pointing at him as she took a step back, 'But I need to hold his hand, so that he knows he's not alone, it isn't fair. Paul needs me, and I can't be there for him.'

Alison stepped forward, 'Paul knows that you loved him. It's not your dad's fault, he wasn't to know that Paul wouldn't be viewable. Come with us and we'll all go for a coffee and try and make sense of all of this. I'm sorry, but the undertaker could have handled things better.' She too reached out her arm for her daughter, but her comfort was also rebuked.

'No mum, he promised me,' retorted Bella.

'But I didn't know love,' pleaded Hamish.

'But you promised,' was all she said as she lowered her hand and then immediately brought it up to wipe her tears. She turned and walked over to Irvine's car and sat in the passenger seat and waited, staring down at her hands all the time.

Irvine, at a loss as to what to do for the best, looked to Alison. She gave a slight nod of encouragement and he took his lead from her. 'I'll take her to my house and make sure she has something to eat and drink and maybe a rest. I'm sure she'll see sense then. You aren't to blame, not at all.' He turned and strode off to his car and slowly drove off.

Alison watched them go and turned to her husband to say soothing words, but all that Hamish could hear was his daughter shouting, 'But you promised.'

Chapter 18

Molly switched on the kettle and took several mugs from the drainer and was drying them as she felt a cold wind rush through the house like a wraith swooshing through a graveyard. She shivered and continued wiping with the tea towel, the draft had indicated that the family had returned. The front door had been opened and a winter chill had dashed through the house to indicate their presence. She finished drying the mugs, placed them next to the teapot and as the kettle finished boiling, Alison walked into the kitchen. Molly poured some boiling water into the pot to warm it and replaced its lid. She turned to Alison, 'I thought you'd all appreciate a nice cup of tea and one of my scones, then I'll disappear. I expect folks will want to start paying their respects. How were things? Did you get to see your Paul?'

Alison slowly shook her head in sorrow, 'The undertaker told us that we couldn't. Paul is too scarred for us to view,' she said slowly, as if the realisation was only just sinking in.

'Oh! That's such a shame. I know that you'd have found it comforting to see him. Though I expect Mr Green knows what he's about. He's buried enough folk around here, including my Bill, God Bless him.' She walked over and embraced her neighbour and good friend.

Alison returned the embrace and said, 'Could you please stick around Molly? If you don't mind. Hamish hasn't said a word on the drive home. I don't think I can face folk, not yet anyway. We've still to go to the registrar's office to register Paul's death, you know, so that the funeral can be properly arranged.'

'Of course, I don't mind. I'll just re-boil this kettle and make that tea. Leave the doorbell for me to answer. I'll ask folk to come back tomorrow, they won't mind. They just want to pay their respects.' She broke off the embrace and walked back to the kettle and fussed over some plates, knives, butter and a pot of jam.

'No need for a plate for Bella, she's gone to Irvine's,' stated Alison ruefully.

'Oh, is she alright, you know, in the circumstances?'

'No, not really,' confided Alison, grateful for someone to talk with. 'She blames her dad, she got angry because he'd promised her that she could hold Paul's hand. She was shouting at him. It's really hurt him, though we both know that grief can make you do irrational things. I'm sure that she'll calm down at Irvine's. He's going to make her something to eat.'

'Och, the poor wee angel. She'll see sense soon enough. It's hit her hard. It's hit you all hard. Your poor Paul, he was such a lovely lad.'

They left the sentiment hanging in the air as they both reminisced in their heads about what Paul had meant to them.

Hamish walked into the room, unknowingly interrupting their reverie. He opened a drawer, below the microwave shelf, and started to pull out bits of shoelaces, string, old keys and some tools. His rummaging broke the silence in the room, and he was so preoccupied that he jumped at the touch of Molly's hand upon his shoulder. He turned around, startled like a thief interrupted by a homeowner switching on a light.

'Forget what you are looking for and come away and sit down. I'd like you to drink this cup of tea and eat one of my scones, it's your favourite cheese topped one,' said Molly as she gently turned him around, towards the kitchen table.

Silently, he walked over to the table and sat down on one of the chairs. He absently picked up his knife and looked to the tip of it, appearing to examine it, like a surgeon poised to make an incision during an operation. He then seemed to make his mind up and sunk it into the butter pot, scooping out a generous amount onto its blade. He then reached over and took a scone, careful to pick it up gently, ensuring that he had both halves, for Molly had thoughtfully pre-cut them for the family. It was still warm from the oven and in normal circumstances he would have relished the warmed, baked treat.

A mug of steaming tea was carefully placed in front of him. The doorbell chimed, interrupting this ritual and both women looked to the other. Molly adamantly pointed to a vacant chair and nodded. Alison sat down as silently bidden and watched her dear friend and neighbour walk out of the kitchen and to the front door.

Hamish waited until she had gone and said quietly, almost conspiratorially, 'I've let her down. I shouldn't have promised, what was I thinking?'

Alison sighed, 'You weren't to know love, and when Bella calms down, she'll see sense.'

'But I know that I let her down. She's never shouted at me like that before,' he put down his knife and scone and pushed his plate away. 'I couldn't save our Paul, his injuries were too severe, and now our Bella is slipping away from us. It's all my fault.'

Alison leaned forward and grasped Hamish by the hand, 'Now you listen to me, you daft lump. I don't need you slipping back into a depression. None of this is your fault. Yes, there was nothing you could do for Paul, no-one could have saved him. Our Bella needs us, no matter what. If she needs to shout at us, against the injustices of the world, then let her. I'd far rather have her shouting at us, at you, than strangers, or her friends, or even Irvine. Because I know that you'll take all that anger from her and turn it into love. You have broad shoulders and a huge heart. She'll come to her senses and realise that not being able to see Paul was not your decision, but was the professional advice of the undertaker, even if he wasn't being professional. I don't know what sort of ego-trip he was on, but we must accept that he wouldn't let any of us view Paul because he wasn't in a fit state to be seen by family. We must remember Paul as he was, our loveable, handsome, fun-loving, caring son. And we all loved him, and he loved us back. That's how I'd like to remember him. That's how you must remember him too.'

Hamish nodded and then burst into huge uncontrollable tears as he reached forward and sobbed into his wife's chest. She held him tight, made soothing noises, as if to a baby, and stroked his hair and allowed him to finally break down. Molly, who had returned from ushering away visitors to the home, watched from the doorway and then immediately tiptoed into their lounge, not wanting to intrude upon this most intimate of moments.

'Come away from the curtain, leave them in peace, they'll want to be left alone at a time like this, and I'd like some quiet from your constant fuss at the window,' deplored Alec to his wife as he ruffled his newspaper for emphasis of his disapproval of her actions. 'It's my day off and I'd like to just sit down and crack on with the crossword in a minute and not have you fretting and worrying over something that is, quite frankly, none of your business.'

Maisie tutted at her husband with impatience, 'That woman hasn't even been in once to see them, and she calls herself a friend. We'd better go across and pay our respects.' She fussed at her hair and smoothed down her dress, never taking her eyes from her window, 'Go and put a shirt and tie on.'

'Is that all you are worried about? What people think of us? Besides, how do you know that she hasn't?' He left the questions hanging in the air. They remained unanswered for several minutes whilst his wife stood watching the house across the street, almost at attention, like a proud Guardsman outside Buckingham Palace, alert to any intruder, before he said, 'Of course, because you've been at the window all morning. Just leave them alone for goodness sake.' He ruffled his newspaper once more and gathered the pages together into a disorderly pile and then reached over to the table beside his armchair and plucked a pencil from a mug that contained various scissors and pens and then stood up and slammed the folded newspaper against his leg, as if to grab her attention. It didn't work.

'I'm away to get some peace and quiet, please come away from there. We'll go across together, once I've finished my crossword.' He stood up and made his way to the bathroom, already engrossed in the first eight-lettered across clue, *'An energetic group out to make mischief.'*

The watcher at the window continued her lonely vigil whilst muttering under her breath, 'Not once have I seen her go into that house, some friend she is.' After a few more minutes, she gave up and reluctantly left her lookout post and made her way upstairs to get changed in the back bedroom.

'I do hope that my Bill has met you and guided you on your new path Paul, you dear boy,' said Molly as she stared up at her extended family's photo. 'And give him my love, I miss him terribly,' she continued as she heard deep, guttural sobs emanate from the kitchen. She tried desperately not to cry, though she'd miss her grandson-like neighbour terribly. She smiled up at him instead, remembering the laughs and merriment that he brought into her life, especially after her Bill died. She thought she'd never find enjoyment again, but Paul soon helped her, in his own daft way.

The sobbing continued, interspersed with low-voiced soothing platitudes from Alison. Molly began to feel that she should leave but was torn between wanting to help the couple and being too intrusive. She smiled once more at Paul's photo, and said, 'You lovely boy, I hope that you are at peace, don't you worry, I'll look after your sister and your parents, I promise you.' She wiped her eyes with her soggy tissue and walked to the lounge door. She hesitated briefly, then, as she heard more heart-torn howling from the kitchen, she opened it as quietly as she could and crept out through to the lobby and out of the inside door. She hoped that the outside door was unlocked and was relieved to find that it opened upon her gentle touch. She looked back towards the kitchen, wishing that she could help in some way, but knowing that nothing could ever take the pain away from these grieving parents. She walked through the outside door and closed it gently behind her, almost deferentially, like an undertaker closing a hearse door at a funeral.

She then turned briskly, knowing that she had a pile of sandwiches to make, and was surprised by two figures on the doorstep. 'Oh, hello Alec and Maisie, sorry, you surprised me there.' She spied Alec's white shirt and black tie under his rain jacket. 'I've just been making sure that Hamish and Alison have had something to eat and drink.'

'Oh, yes, well,' stuttered Maisie as she looked red-faced. Alec bobbed up and down on the balls of his feet. Like a pleased police officer watching a disgruntled father giving a son a telling off for some low-level crime, whilst giving his wife an '*I told you so,*' look. He soon realised how inappropriate his movements and look would be and stopped, for fear that his wife would clout him one and be disagreeable all day. Fortunately, she was too ashamed at her earlier thoughts to give her husband any heed.

Molly interjected upon their thoughts and insisted, 'It's best to leave them alone for another day. They are, as you can imagine, so distraught. It's only just hit Hamish. He's been so stoical and looked after Alison and Bella, but now it's his turn to have some tender care. But don't worry, I've been popping through from around the back-door. I've a key, you see.'

'Ah,' began Maisie, unsure of what to say, her face was of a deeper scarlet now.

Alec took the lead, as well as the moral high-ground, 'Bless you Molly, what a great friend you are indeed.' He nodded to his wife, 'We'll be off then, we'll come back tomorrow night, after my work, won't we Maisie.' He looked firmly at his wife, defying her to challenge him.

Maisie looked sheepishly up to him, nodded briefly and asked of Molly, 'Do they need anything, what can I bring?'

'Nothing really, Isaac from the shop has provided enough tea, coffee, milk, sugar, bread, fillings and biscuits. He's been so generous.' Molly ushered them off the doorstep and the couple obediently walked down the steps. 'I've a fresh batch of scones in the oven and I'll make some cakes this afternoon. I'm making their favourites, you know, to give them some sort of comfort. It's important to eat at a time like this. I'll pop them around the back again. I don't want to be too intrusive. If Alison and Hamish aren't in the kitchen, then I'll just leave them on the table.'

Alec nodded sagely, whilst his wife looked down at the driveway, abashed, as she allowed herself to be reluctantly led off.

Hamish had cried and yelled himself to fatigue. He could cry no more for the cherished son that he'd lost. He patted his wife's back and broke off from her tight grip. 'I loved him,' he simply said.

'I know love, we all did. And he loved you. I'm glad that you've finally cried yourself out. You need to cry at any time you feel like it. Don't bottle it up, let it all out, we've had the most catastrophic thing happen to us, and only we can know the pain that we are in.'

Hamish wiped his tears and running nose as best he could with his hand and then lent forward and gave his wife a delicate kiss. 'I love you.'

Alison smiled warmly, 'And I love you.'

'We have to start arranging things, do you want me to do it, you know, the registrar?'

'No. I think it best that we do things together.'

'Okay,' he broke off the embrace and reached for his phone. He also pulled out the pieces of paper that Brendan had given him. 'I'll phone up for an appointment, I think that's what we have to do.'

'Alright, but I think straight after your call you should eat the rest of that scone. I'll just use the toilet, then I'll make us a nice cup of tea, these ones look a bit cold.'

Hamish nodded, fighting back fresh tears as he imagined how cold his son's body would now be without life-affirming blood pumping around it, providing warmth and nutrients.

Alison nodded back and briskly left the room, her bladder had been protesting its fullness for some time and there hadn't been an appropriate time to leave a distraught Bella or Hamish.

Hamish dialled the number on the slip of paper, it was picked up on the second ring. 'Hello, is that the registrar,' he enquired, not realising that he'd interrupted her introduction.

'Yes, hello, I'm Cassandra, how can I help you?'

'I'd like to register the death of my son please. The undertaker gave me a piece of paper for you.'

'Oh. I'm so sorry to hear that you've lost your son,' she replied in a lower voice.

'Thank you, I don't know what we have to do, I've never done this before. I've only registered births before, and that was when I was serving overseas, the army admin office took care of things.'

'Well, it's a bit like that, if you come down to the council offices, do you know where that is?' she gently asked.

'Yes, by the town car park?'

'Yes, that's us. Normally you'd go to Reception and wait in a queue. But we don't have any weddings today. So, me and my colleague are at a loose-end for a few hours. I am training her, she is qualified, but is new to our office. It's her first day, but I'll be there too. If you enter the building and take a first right, through the closed double-doors and wait in the area there, I'll keep an eye out for you. But please don't rush. You have a few days to do it, only come if you feel up to it.'

'No, no, I think it best that my wife, Alison, and I do it. It needs to be done and there is no point in delaying it. I understand that the undertakers can't make any funeral arrangements without another slip of paper that you give us?'

'Yes, I'm afraid he can't do much until he gets the signed death certificate from us. I'm so sorry.'

'Thank you for fitting us in, we'll drive straight over, see you soon.'

'I'll look out for you both, Mr...'

'I'm so sorry, I didn't introduce myself. My head's all over the place. Mr Dewart, Hamish.'

'Okay Hamish, please don't rush, come over when you feel up to it. Bye bye.'

Hamish fumbled with his phone, working out where the disconnect call button was. It was a long-running family joke that he couldn't work his mobile very well. He wished that his son was here to help him. He just wished his son was here. Satisfied that he'd got the right button he then slipped the phone into his left front trouser pocket. He then walked over to the odds and ends drawer once more and fumbled around. 'Gotcha,' he declared and dropped the item into his other pocket and closed the drawer. He walked back to the chair, sat down and toyed with his plate as he let his mind wander down a dark, lonely pathway once more.

Alison walked in, unknowingly interrupting his morose thoughts once again. 'Gosh, I really needed that. I'll pop the kettle on. How did you get on, I heard you talking, did you get through to the registrar?'

'Yes, she sounded a nice old lady, just what folks like us need at a time like this. She said to follow the instructions on the slip of paper and to come anytime in the next few hours.'

'I guess few folks want to get married at this time of year, and all the Christmas babies are born in September.'

Hamish smiled and was about to say something, but his Alison beat him to it.

'Just like the baby boom after Operations, when you lads and lassies come home to us waiting spouses and partners. Six months away from home builds up a fair appetite!'

Hamish smiled wider again and said, 'Yep, nine months after coming home from Bosnia, our Paul popped out!'

Alison smiled briefly and said, 'He was a great son, wasn't he? He didn't deserve this, not our Paul.'

Hamish walked over to her and enveloped her in a tight hug, 'No, no he didn't. I just wish that I could get my hands on that driver.'

'I know, but don't. Don't even think about that. We need you here, not in some jail. Let the police and the courts deal with him, for what it's worth. Drunk drivers never seem to get a heavy sentence. Oh Hamish, I don't want to think about what's to come, what happens if the driver gets away with it?'

'I don't know, I just don't know. I think we should just take each day as it comes. We should concentrate on our Bella and giving Paul a great funeral, for us and his friends.'

'And your family and mine, for his grandparents, uncles and aunties too.'

Hamish thought grimly back to when he last saw his father and mother and quickly changed the subject as he let go from the hug, 'I fair need a pee myself. Shall we have a cuppa before we go?'

'Yes, love, and we'd better finish a scone or two, Molly has gone out the front. She'll be so upset if we don't finish her home-bakes. And I think we both should have full tummies so that we can concentrate and give Paul a good funeral. I don't trust that Brendan, what an awful manner he had.'

'Yes, and yet, folks around here really praise him, saying he's the best undertaker in town.'

'He's the only undertaker in town. Perhaps we should have used the other firm, it's only fifteen miles away.'

'I know he was insensitive, but so long as he cares for Paul's body, that's all that matters. I really need to pee now.'

Alison motioned him away with her hands and once he left the room, she let out a long sigh and switched the kettle on. Molly had thoughtfully already filled it up for the next round of teas.

Chapter 19

The Saltire flag waved proudly over the three-storey building and with each furl and snap of the material in the wind the tethered rope rubbed against the flagpole in boastfulness of its anchorage. In contrast the flagpole swayed in rhythmic motion to the strong gusts that swept across from the North Sea. The water looked rough and Hamish pitied the ships crews that had to work against nature's displeasure. He was glad that he'd joined an Army that favoured land, rather than the Royal Navy. His stomach had always protested sudden movements, especially on rollercoasters like at Legoland when the children were younger. He thought that it would be a sedate day out, looking at large-scale brick models. He hadn't expected violent rides that his children loved, more especially when they saw the discomfort of their father and his growing nausea with each new attraction that tossed him about.

'Are you up to this Hamish?' asked a concerned Alison.

'Yes, sorry, I was away with the fairies again. I was admiring the flag. I always thought that being back home in Scotland would keep us all happy and safe.'

'And we were, well until that drunk man…'

He reached out for his wife's hand and was relieved to feel its strong grip on his. 'Let's start looking after Paul, in the only way we can now. He pushed the door open and they walked through together.

The smell of stale alcohol from the man finger-pointing at the young receptionist assailed their nostrils. They ignored them both. Let others care about them, they simultaneously thought. They slipped past, unnoticed by the man moaning at the cost of his council tax to the inattentive ears of someone who'd heard this familiar story before, plenty of money for the local boozer, but none to spare for his

contribution to society. How did he think street lights,

refuse collection and other vital services got paid? Her

glazed-over eyes demonstrated that this was just one of

many beleaguered customers that she'd seen already today.

If only pubs didn't open until the evening, like in the good

old days that her nan talked about. She continued to

pretend to be listening, trying to edge into the conversation

with the council's viewpoint.

The bereaved couple went through the double doors, to

the privileged inner sanctum of the local council, and were

relieved to find that the closing of the doors afforded a

noise barrier from the drunk, and protection from the

fumes he emanated from his rank breath and body odour.

They quietly walked to the chairs and sat down.

Hamish looked around him, squinting at the door signs,

trying to work out which office belonged to the registrar.

He vowed to listen to what his wife and children had been saying weeks earlier, and he'd book an eye test soon. Children. *'Should he still be saying plural or singular?'* he thought. He didn't think he could start saying child. They'd been born eighteen months apart and were as thick as thieves. Always playing together and taking the mickey out of their father. He always thought of them, rather than him or her. How could he bring himself to tell people, when they asked, that he only had a daughter? It's one of the first questions that patients asked of their nurse when trying to find common ground, to make polite conversation when a nurse was carrying out intimate tasks. That would be a great conversation stopper, wouldn't it? Having to explain to burdened patients that he'd lost a son. They didn't need that additional load on their encumbered lives. They needed a nurse to take their heavy weight from them, not to add to it with his own sorrows. He doubted that he'd nurse again, how could he enter once more to the caring profession? He knew that he'd have to hang up his tunic for good. Besides, he'd need to be there for Bella and Alison, they had a long, lonely road to walk up together.

Alison pointed to an office. 'I think it's that one.'

He looked, glad for something new to think about. He couldn't make out the writing, but agreed anyway, with a nod of his head.

Alison looked to him, knowing that he couldn't make out the writing, but knowing too, that this was not the time to be chastising him over his refusal to acknowledge his failing eyesight and his need for distance spectacles.

'Should we knock?' she suggested. She had seen two ladies in the office, sat by opposite desks.

'Let's give it a few minutes. This'll be the first time we've told anyone outside of our friends and family. Will you speak for me, you know, if I have one of my moments?'

'You know I will love, I always have and always will do,' she answered as she held his hand once more. She'd grown used to his disassociated spells over the years. It was part and parcel of him after discovering that he had Post Traumatic Stress. She refused to call it a Disorder because she knew him to have done brave things over the years, things that would have had people turning, running off, screaming for their mothers. Instead, he had run to the things that now caused his sleeping nightmares and waking detachments. He relived events during the day and had learnt to acknowledge them, to let them play out, to pass on and then to accept them as heroic, past events that he had done and would no longer be expected to do. He had told her about these day-visions, and they had agreed to call them his moments, for he just needed a moment, alone with his thoughts and to perform his coping mechanisms.

'I love you.'

'And I you,' she replied as the office door opened.

A tall, thin woman dressed in matching skirt and jacket stepped out. She looked surprised to see them, sat there, patiently. 'Who are you?' she primly asked.

'Mr and Mrs Dewart,' replied Hamish getting to his feet. He offered up his hand to shake, 'Paul's parents.'

She looked down her spectacles that had fallen from the bridge of her nose at the proffered hand, as if it had pus-filled bandages wrapped around it. She wrinkled her nose, either at the human contact, or to halt the slippage motion of her glasses. 'And who is Paul?'

'Our son, he died. Are you Cassandra? We spoke on the phone, about thirty minutes ago.'

'Ah, I see, no, I am Rachel, another of the registrars. How may I help you?'

Hamish and Alison looked to each other, not quite believing the aloofness and insensitivity of this public official.

Hamish broke off the look and met the eye of the official as he lowered his still ignored hand. 'As I've said, our son, Paul, has died, and we need to register his death.'

'Yes, I understand that, but you haven't made an appointment, have y…'

'I'm so sorry, Mr and Mrs Dewart, I've been on an important call since the minute I took yours,' interrupted Cassandra, the head registrar. 'I need to get back to it, but I'll hand you over to my colleague, Rachel. She'll help you. I'm so, so sorry to learn of Paul's passing, please come into the office.' She ushered them into a room that overlooked the town's harbour. Through the partially-opened blinds the couple could make out a large trawler unloading its catch. That'll be why there were few seagulls by this building thought Alison, they'll be waiting for their lunch there.

'Please sit down, by Rachel's desk,' guided Cassandra with her outstretched palms. She smiled warmly as the couple sat down. 'I'm so sorry I wasn't around to meet you nor had the time to leave a note on Rachel's desk. I'll leave you in her capable hands and just finish this call.' She walked over to the adjacent desk, picked up the phone, and spoke quietly into it.

Rachel came around her desk and sat down and faced the couple, then looked to her computer screen.

Hamish and Alison braced themselves for another *'sorry for your loss'* response and were taken aback when they received a harsh, 'Can I have the slip of paper from the undertaker?'

A hand shot out from behind the desk, urgently demanding to receive the necessary paperwork.

Hamish fumbled with several slips of paper and finally just handed them all to the abrupt woman.

She took them from him and selected one, as if from a packet of cards during a magic trick. She handed the others back. 'Those are for you, they are your instructions from the undertaker. Did you read them?'

Hamish was about to answer when the lady immediately asked another question.

'Can I have his birth certificate,' she demanded.

Hamish hesitated, 'Er, his birth certificate?'

'Yes, his birth certificate,' she repeated, as if a parent speaking to a wayward child.

'Hold the line a moment please,' whispered Cassandra into the telephone. She then clasped it to her shoulder, to smother any noise. 'Rachel needs Paul's birth certificate to register Paul's death. There is information on it that she needs. It's on the list of things to bring that the undertaker gave you Mr Dewart,' she gently said.

'Ah, sorry, I didn't read it fully.'

Rachel rolled her eyes heavenwards.

Her colleague spoke quickly, on her behalf. 'Not to worry, it's easily done. I'm sure Rachel can manage without it. It's just a formality, easily navigated around. Isn't it, Rachel?' She beamed encouragingly to her colleague.

Rachel tutted. 'It's highly irregular, the guidelines say that we need it.'

Alison turned to Hamish, 'It'll be somewhere in Paul's room, but I don't want to disturb anything. I wouldn't know where to start looking,' she beseeched.

'Can we go home and get it for you. Maybe come back in a day or two? Or, perhaps after the weekend? I'm sure we can find it between us.'

Rachel's glasses slipped down her nose again, giving her a stern headmistress look as she glanced first to Alison and then to Hamish. Her eyes stayed on him as she strictly said, 'It is a legal requirement to register a death within seven days. We usually need the birth certificate, but I have this information from the mortuary via your undertaker.' She waved the piece of paper, as if fanning herself to cool down the situation. 'I can get everything else online, from our central registry.' She looked back to her computer and typed away.

Alison and Hamish looked to the other and shrugged, just another oddity in a surreal turn of events.

'Could you please confirm where your son was born, I don't understand it.'

'RAF Akrotiri, I was serving with the…'

'So Akrotiri is the name of a country?' interrupted the registrar.

'No, it's Royal Air Force…'

'Yes, yes, I understand the RAF bit,' said Rachel impatiently. 'I've never heard of the country Akrotiri. I've found in my short time as a registrar that military administration is very lazy. They should have typed his town of birth onto his birth certificate. I have the copy here, on my screen.'

'That was Paul's place of birth. The airbase was called Akrotiri, it's in Cyprus,' replied Hamish firmly.

'I see. Thank you.' Rachel continued to type away, ignoring the couple before them. She began a serious of tuts and huffs of breath.

Cassandra finished her call with a whispered, 'goodbye, see you at the next heads meeting,' and replaced the handset. She looked across and gave a friendly smile and offered, 'I'm so sorry about this, urgent business, but I can help now. Legally Rachel must finish the registration,' she explained. She looked over to her colleague, concern was now etched upon Cassandra's face.

Rachel picked up her phone and pressed a speed-dial number, it was soon answered. 'May I speak to Doctor Penrose?' She paused for a moment and then pompously said, 'I am the registrar for the North East section, I need to confirm some information.'

Another pause played out, allowing time for Hamish and Alison to stretch out their hands and find the others for support.

'Hello Doctor, you forgot to sign the post-mortem and body release form. I cannot proceed with the registration of Paul Dewart's death without it.'

Alison gave a sharp gasp and her pallor whitened.

Hamish squeezed her hand, as if to pump blood through her body and for support.

Ignorant to the feelings of the parents Rachel proceeded with, 'It's highly irregular, but I'll note the time of this call and yes, if you'd amend it with a digital signature within the next few minutes, then I can proceed.' She put the phone down, without a thank you or goodbye.

She turned her computer screen around so that the couple before her could read it. 'These are Paul's injuries and his cause of death, could you confirm these facts?'

Hamish quickly let go of his wife's hands and whirled the screen back to the registrar.

She tutted, louder this time, and then swivelled it back to him, like a ghoulish game of pass the parcel. 'I do need you to read it and confirm,' she insisted.

Hamish turned it back to her, though stopped it at the halfway point. 'I'm trying to save my wife from further upset. She doesn't need to read this, does she?' he angrily retorted.

Rachel sat back in her seat and immediately stood to rose. She felt a delicate hand on her shoulder as she was joined by Cassandra who gently pushed her back into her seat. 'Mr Dewart can read it himself, can't he Rachel. There is no need to upset Mrs Dewart anymore than she already is.'

Rachel scowled and shrugged her left shoulder, to brush off the restraining hand.

Hamish wished that Rachel had taken that urgent phone call instead and that this kindly older lady had seen to them. He patted his wife on the knee and rested his hand there for her support as he read the screen. He too grew paler and paler as he silently read of his son's injuries and his cause of death. He nodded to the registrars.

'It's for the death certificate. I have to type out a cause of death and inform you of it before I print and sign it,' explained Rachel.

'I'm so sorry, Mr and Mrs Dewart, this is never an easy process,' she looked discouragingly at her new colleague. She kept her thoughts to herself but made a mental note that perhaps and despite her training, maybe Rachel wasn't cut out for this job and should be assigned another role within the council, perhaps one with no contact with people, just computers.

A ping from the computer interrupted her thoughts. Hamish nodded and said, 'Yes, I understand and agree. I saw the accident site. Those injuries are consistent with what I saw.'

Rachel turned sharply to him and began, 'How on earth did you get to see...'

'That can't have been easy Mr Dewart, I'm sure the police looked after you and took you away, perhaps saw you home?' interjected Cassandra.

'Yes, I drove home, there wasn't anything I could do. I had to see for myself.'

'As any father would have,' said Cassandra soothingly.

'I now have a digital signature,' explained Rachel, 'and can issue you with a death certificate.' She typed a bit more and then the printer broke into life and whirred away. Cassandra took the paper from the tray and handed it to Hamish. 'Please take this to the undertaker so that he can legally proceed. If you require any additional copies, for instance for an insurance company, then I can print them now, or later, for ten pounds each.'

'Oh, I don't think Paul had insurance,' mumbled Alison, still upset from seeing her son's post-mortem results. 'I'll have to go through his things, maybe check with his bank. Oh, we have so much to do, and I've forgotten my purse.'

Hamish patted her knee again, withdrew his hand and felt in his pocket. 'My wallet is another thing I forgot, we'll come back if we need more copies.' He turned to Cassandra, 'Thank you for your help.'

Cassandra nodded, capturing his meaning as he looked across to Rachel and then stood up and guided his wife out of the office. He didn't bother closing the door after them and they walked past a young couple, cooing at their baby as the proud new mother rocked the pram back and forth. Alison and Hamish then walked straight out of the double doors and past the reception where the drunk was now sat looking sheepish next to a burly security guard.

Chapter 20

'That was awful Hamish, she had no ounce of compassion. She's not good at her job. She sees people at the worst time of their lives, as well as their happiest. Imagine how dour she must be when happy parents are trying to register a birth. Or at weddings, is she the proverbial spectre at the feast? She had no sensitivity. I didn't need to read about all those injuries Paul sustained. You know I didn't want to know. I'll now be imagining all the pain he must have been in. It's in my head and now it's all I can think about. What an awful woman.'

'I know lass, I know,' consoled Hamish. 'I don't think she'll be doing that job much longer. I'm sure that Cassandra will see to that. I think she was a recent trainee. I tried to save you from seeing the screen.'

Alison stopped walking and turned into an embrace which Hamish reciprocated. They held each other tightly as the world continued around them. An elderly woman, walking past with her tartan shopping trolley rolling obediently behind her, smiled, failed to see their tears, mistook the cuddling and thought how loving the couple looked.

'Can we go to our Paul now, please Hamish. I need to sit by his coffin and say some long-forgotten prayers. I just hope that there is a heaven and that our son is safe and pain-free. I hope that he is looking down upon us.'

'Of course, I'll drive us straight there. I'm sure that Brendan and his son have finished what they must do and have made Paul comfortable in his coffin. I know that he showed little sensitivity as well, but I'm certain that he is proficient at what he does. I'm sure that Paul is already in one of his rooms where we can close the door and have some quiet time with our lad. Should we ask our Bella to come too? I'm sure that Irvine won't mind driving her back to the funeral home.'

'No, she needs to have something to eat and perhaps a sleep. You know that deep down she doesn't blame you for anything?'

Hamish gave an imperceptible nod of his head.

'None of this is your fault, I need you to show me that you agree and that you know that you have not broken any promises.'

'But Bella said I did,' he began.

Alison interrupted him, 'But deep down she knows that it was out of your control. And deep down you know that it wasn't your fault.'

'Yes,' replied Hamish though his face betrayed his true feelings.

The bereaved couple had driven in silence to the undertakers and were now sat in the stilled car, facing the building. There was a familiar feeling of dread in the pit of Hamish's stomach. It was the same dread he felt in the past when going into emergency situations in the army. The feelings had followed him into civilian life as he battled his PTSD, and now he was aware of that familiar hold on his intestines and groin. Yet, he was confused as to why it was dogging him so now. There shouldn't be any fear or trepidation, he was about to do a fatherly thing. A frown visibly crossed his face.

Alison interrupted his dark thoughts as she reached over to grasp the back of his left hand. He had not relinquished his hold on the handbrake, and she could see his hand getting whiter as his grip got tighter. 'Shall we go in then love?'

'Aye, lass, let's see our boy,' he said determinedly as his right hand reached up to his chest, as if to relieve an itch.

They both exited the car and quietly closed their doors. Hamish locked the car, already missing the Batman keyring. He locked the car with the key and gave a brief grin as he thought how Paul would have laughed at this action. It was another long-standing family joke that Hamish never used the electronic button on the key. He was a die-hard who still used the actual metal key to lock his car, not truly trusting to technology. He allowed the grin to fall and walked to the front of the vehicle to be with his wife who waited patiently at the flag-stoned walkway, where some low-level lighting rods shone dimly on this dark day and cast lights onto the well-trimmed hedging from which bird chatter and movement emanated. He reached for her hand, more to comfort him from this dread feeling, than to succour her.

They walked wordlessly to the entrance and Alison reached the door first and opened it and ushered him in. She allowed the door to close by itself and was distracted by how silently it closed.

The stillness in the building seemed almost eerie as the couple waited patiently in the unmanned reception area. It threatened to overwhelm Hamish as he struggled to go through his breathing exercises to try and rid himself of his anxiety. He felt in his pocket for his talisman that he used in such situations, to give himself something to physically feel, to hold and ground himself. He just felt the car key, his keyring was now with his superhero, his Paul. He turned to Alison, his rock, and grasped her hand. She smiled up at him and kept to herself how surprised she was to feel that his palm was sweaty and that she thought his breathing was laboured. She remembered his chest rubbing in the car and was about to say something when a rasping voice broke the peace she was briefly feeling.

'Hello, hello, Mr and Mrs Dewart, we weren't expecting you. Most folk phone first before coming,' he chastised. His eyebrows raised, drawing Alison's eyes away from his wheezing mouth. She was temporarily distracted by the undertaker, all thoughts of her husband's health shelved for the moment.

'Hello again Brendan, we thought it best that you have Paul's death certificate as soon as possible. You know, so that his funeral can be arranged. So that we can give family and friends a date and time.' She turned and smiled to Hamish. He looked lost in thought, so she reached over to his right hand and gently took from him the piece of paper that he was holding. She passed it to Brendan who took it eagerly. She looked down at the document and his hand and shivered at the thought of his dirty and heavily nicotine-stained fingers caring for her Paul, who had always been so smartly turned out.

'Thank you. I shall be able to proceed with the administration this afternoon and will telephone you later.' He took a step forward, as if to open the outside door for the couple.

'May we please sit with our Paul? Have you made him comfortable?'

Brendan pursed his lips, as if deciding. 'Yes,' he finally said after a few moments thought and a brief glance up to the clock in the office, through the glassed frontage. 'Yes, my son has seen to Paul, as you say, your boy is now comfortable in his coffin. He is resting in one of our rooms.'

'So, can we please sit with him?' pursued Alison.

'Yes, though it's highly irregular. As I say, most folk telephone before coming.' He appeared to be making his mind up. 'I do have to remind you though that Paul's funeral will have to be a closed casket one. You won't be able to view your son. It's for your own peace of mind. He was heavily scarred by the accident and subsequent tests.'

'You mean when he was shunted by that low life,' began Hamish, now out of his reverie. He made to continue his statement, but Alison stilled him with a squeeze of the hand she was still holding until she knew that Hamish no longer needed it.

'Yes, well, of course you can go in and see your son's coffin. I'll show you the way.'

'And sit with him,' insisted Alison, as they obediently followed the undertaker.

'But of course, Mrs Dewart. There are several chairs there. 'Will it just be the two of you?'

'Yes, we haven't made any arrangements with Bella. She's likely to be the only person to want to see Paul's coffin before the funeral. But she is with her fiancé just now. She'll not come until tomorrow. I'll make sure she phones you first.'

Ahead of them, Brendan smiled. 'Thank you.' He reached a room with the number 1 on the door. 'Paul is just in here, in our best room, resting comfortably,' he said, with what he hoped would be a reassuring smile. He entered and ushered the couple in.

Alison walked in first and gave a small gasp and said, 'Oh my dear boy,' and walked straight to the coffin and wrapped her arms around the smooth wood. Hamish went in after her and placed a comforting hand on her shoulder.

'I'm so sorry for your loss Mr and Mrs Dewart.'

'Thank you,' replied Hamish in a low voice as he turned to face the undertaker. 'Can we take some time to be with our Paul please?'

'But of course, my son and I will be about, just let either of us know if we are needed.' Brendan gave an almost imperceptible bow as he made to turn. 'It does get hot in here, so I'll leave the door open.'

'Not to worry, we are both very cold after being outside. I'll close the door after you. Alison wants to say some prayers over Paul's coffin. She'll want a bit of privacy.'

A frown creased Brendan's forehead as he wheezed in a harsh breath. 'Mmm, but of course, do wait at reception if you need either of us.'

'Thank you, Brendan,' replied Hamish as he watched the undertaker leave. He quietly closed the door and walked back to his wife. Alison was still draped over Paul's coffin, sobbing uncontrollably. Hamish reached out and cuddled her from behind. He remained silent, for he knew that no words could console her. Just as she had allowed him to ride out his tears and rage in their kitchen, earlier that day, so he had to now allow her to let out this bout of deep sorrow.

After a few minutes his eyes were drawn around the room, it was plainly decorated and was furnished with basic wooden chairs with deep ornate blue cushions sunk into the seat and back. By Paul's coffin, on the side wall, was a tiled backdrop displaying what looked like a kneeling, bearded and robed figure of Jesus. On his shoulder rested a hand from a taller figure who had wings upon his back. The stereotypical depiction of Jesus with an angel helping him to ascend to heaven. He so wished that he could believe that his son was in a better place, was at peace. But his son was at peace, before the drunk driver had entered his life, his life was peaceful and happy.

Hamish allowed his rage to play out and dissipate by looking at the tall flowers in the large vase below the tiled scenery. He was never good at naming them, but he studied their beauty and allowed their scent to fill his nostrils and wash calmness over him. He studied their petals, admiring the natural beauty before him. An object within them caught his eye and just before his eyes narrowed to focus on it, Alison stopped her sobbing and made to stand up. Hamish released his grip on her. 'I don't know what to say love. It's not natural that our Paul has gone first.'

They both straightened up and remained standing in front of Paul's coffin, unsure of what they should do next. This environment and situation felt so unwanted, alien and out with their control. Alison took out a tissue from her pocket, wiped her eyes and blew her nose. 'I don't know how we can go on without him. But we must try and find a way, for Bella's sake.'

'Aye, love, that we must, though my heart feels fit to burst.'

Alison turned to him with concern. 'Do you have chest pain? I saw you feel around your chest in the car. Is your jaw or arms sore?'

Hamish smiled. 'Don't you worry about me lass, I'm made of strong stuff. We both are, aren't we?'

He saw her nod as she turned back to Paul's coffin, Alison said, 'I know we had our doubts about Brendan, but this room looks beautiful and those flowers are such a nice touch. I was worried that there might be unpleasant smells, you know, from our Paul. Not worried for us, we've smelt some bad things in our line of work, but for Bella. But those flowers hide any smells.'

Hamish turned to the flowers, intent for a closer look, but his attention was distracted once more by an exclamation from his wife.

'Oh no!' she cried. 'I take back all I said about that awful undertaker, look at the brass plate on our boy's coffin. He couldn't even get that right for us.'

Hamish looked back to his son's coffin and read the dates and Paul's full name, checking it for spelling mistakes. He found none, but then saw it. No wonder Alison was so upset. There was a huge scratch below the engraving, as if the engraver had forgotten to lift his tool and had left the machine to do its own bidding.

'I know that few people will see it and that he's to be buried soon. But if he can't get the basics right, what else has he done badly. Is it too late to change undertakers do you think?'

'I think so. I just can't understand why everyone in this area says how good he is. When we leave, I shall ask him to redo it. I expect that they have a special machine in their workrooms so that they can do the plates themselves. It can quickly be rectified.' He ran his hand over his son's coffin and rested it over where his son's cheek would be. He lingered there, making his mind up and turned to his wife and placed his hands over her shoulders.

She looked up, eyes still moist from her tears. She smiled briefly at him.

Hamish didn't return the smile. 'You know we acknowledged that we both are made of strong stuff.'

He waited until he saw her nodding, before he continued. 'We've done some unpleasant things and seen some awful sights. We touched, held and carried some terrible bodies and even body parts. Nursing has seen us do some distasteful duties.'

'Yes, we both have, but you especially. Are you okay? Is this too much for you?'

Hamish shook his head grimly. 'I'm fine. I have an idea.'

Chapter 21

'I wasn't rubbing my chest in pain Alison, I was checking that I still had this,' said Hamish as he withdrew a flat-headed screwdriver from the inside of his jacket pocket.

'Oh,' exclaimed a puzzled Alison.

'Yes, don't you see. I think I should unscrew Paul's coffin and lift the lid and have a look at him first. Then if I think that he looks okay, we can spend some time seeing Paul. Don't you see, we can even hold his hand.'

Alison's eyes widened. She took a step back, almost as if Hamish was holding a knife and was about to stab her. 'I think we should allow Brendan to be the judge. We should accept his professional opinion. Now that I've had to read about Paul's injuries, I'm not sure that I want to see him like that. I want to remember him just like he was, our happy-go-lucky beautiful boy.'

'That's why I want to look in first, let me decide whether you and Bella should see Paul.'

'But you've seen enough trauma, don't see our boy like that,' argued Alison.

'But we only have Brendan's word for it. What if he's being lazy and hasn't done his job properly. Is his son even around to help him. What if they are cutting corners?'

'I don't think they can nowadays. Isn't the funeral industry highly regulated?'

'Aye, well, we've worked in enough highly regulated nursing homes to know that there are still some rotten apples out there and that owners cut corners to try and save money to line their own pockets.'

'But what if Paul is highly scarred, or if his body has already broken down? Please don't do it Hamish. Trust Brendan's judgement.'

'But that's it, don't you see. I don't trust him. He's so cavalier and insensitive. Besides, he should have embalmed Paul to stop his body breaking down. Paul should look like he is just asleep.'

Alison said nothing, she was trying to make sense of this sudden turn in events.

Hamish took her by the hand and led her to the seats. He sat down and encouraged her to do the same. He was still holding the screwdriver and was fiddling about with it, as if he too was trying to come to a decision.

'You sit here with your back to Paul or close your eyes. I'll unscrew the lid and gently open it and peek in. If Paul smells and looks alright, then I'll leave the lid open and we can say our goodbyes to him properly. Like parents should be able to. I want to kiss our boy goodnight one last time. I need to hold him and tell him that I love him.'

'I know that you do, we both do,' replied Alison, biting her lip. 'Okay, but I can't turn my back on Paul. I'll sit here, close my eyes and pray. I know we aren't church-goers, but I need to believe that Paul is in heaven and being looked after.' She patted his hands and closed her eyes.

Hamish looked at her in wonder, at how serene she suddenly looked, as if gathering inner peace from the God that she was so desperate to still believe in. He also saw how beautiful she was too, not just in physical appearance, but in her repose, as a person. He counted himself so lucky in this, so unfortunate an occasion. Yes, they must find a way to go on, for their daughter's sake, he silently affirmed. He watched her lips move in a long-forgotten prayer and felt a pang of jealousy at her innocent belief in an unseen entity.

He rose and walked to his son's coffin. He patted it twice, as if for luck, or to reassure himself that he could do this. He swapped the screwdriver to his right hand, ready to unscrew the coffin lid. He studied the eight screws, trying to find how to take off their ornate plume-like tops, so that he could see their metal screws. He hoped that they would be traditional flat-slotted screws, rather than Phillips, for he hadn't found one of those screwdrivers in the kitchen drawer and hadn't had the opportunity to go down to the shed. He gave one of the screws at the foot of the coffin a tentative push to see if the ornate plumes just lifted off. It gave a gentle unscrew and Hamish laughed, despite himself.

Alison jumped up from her seat, eyes wide and praying forgotten, 'What is it, does he look okay, can I see him now?'

Hamish turned, laughing now vanished. 'I'm sorry love, I've been silly.'

Alison looked at the closed coffin lid and Hamish's empty hands. The screwdriver rested on Paul's coffin and there were no screws. In fact. the coffin looked undisturbed. 'Have you changed your mind?' she gently asked, taking Hamish's hands. She looked hopefully into his eyes, she really didn't want to see her disfigured son.

'No lass. I'm sorry, I got it all wrong.'

Alison's shoulders visibly dropped as she sighed in relief. 'That's okay, let's just sit here for a while and then go and see our Bella.'

Hamish shook his head and took his hands from hers. He reached up for the screwdriver. 'Don't you see?' he asked as he put it back into his pocket.

Alison shook her head, 'I don't know what you mean,' she said looking puzzled.

Hamish pointed to the plume heads, 'These aren't traditional screws. Or at least they look like traditional coffin screw covers.' He twisted around the nearest screw until it unfurled a small amount. 'I didn't need to worry about sneaking a screwdriver past Brendan. They simply unscrew with a gentle twist. And though they look like metal, they are hard plastic.'

'Oh,' was all that Alison could say.

Hamish took her hands and led her back to her seat. 'I think it was probably in my army days when I last said the Lord's Prayer. Why don't you sit here and say it for us? I've forgotten the words. Say it to yourself, or aloud, whichever you prefer.' He withdrew from her hands and watched her close her eyes once more.

Alison mouthed the words silently, she wanted to hear what Hamish was doing.

Hamish breathed in long and hard, gaining resolve and strength to do what he was driven by paternal need to do. He rose again and walked silently back to Paul and began unscrewing the plastic screws, carefully placing each one into his pocket. As the final one was put away, he ran his fingers along the length of Paul's coffin, as if admiring the grain of the wood. He hesitated. His heart was racing. He wondered if he was doing the right thing. He briefly looked guiltily at the door. Then he looked towards the flowers, creased his brow and turned away, puzzled. He saw the depictions of Jesus and the angel and then looked back towards his wife. They had to know. He opened the lid. 'Oh God!' he exclaimed.

Chapter 22

Hamish quickly closed the lid. He put his hands firmly on it. His hands started to shake. He kept repeating 'Oh God!' over and over, like a mantra to a newly-discovered deity.

Alison immediately ceased her praying. Her God was now forgotten. She rushed to Hamish's side and tried to remove his hands, but he pushed down firmly.

'What is it, what's wrong?'

'Why would you, why would he, I don't, I mustn't,' he rambled on incoherently.

Alison took her hands from her son's coffin and placed them on Hamish's shoulders. She shook them. He would not let go of his hold of the coffin lid. 'What is it? Tell me?' she ordered. She ducked and weaved her head, trying to gain her husband's attention. Their eyes finally focused on each other, like a fighter jet's missile locked on a target.

'Slow down Hamish. Catch your breathing. Listen to me. Just breathe. Don't say anything, just breathe. That's it. Keep quiet, just breathe away.' She inhaled loudly and exhaled so that he could hear her and copy her rhythmic breathing. She kept the pace slow and regular and watched patiently, though her soul was screaming out to know what had distressed him so, as he eventually calmed down enough to risk being questioned.

After a few moments she saw his grip on their son's coffin relinquish. His fingers quickly turned from a white knuckled grip back to a pink hue. She took her hands from his shoulders and then turned quickly to Paul's coffin and tried to open the lid.

Hamish slammed his hands down, 'NO!' he hissed. You mustn't look. It's awful. I don't understand. In the field he looked whole. Why would this happen.'

'I don't know what you mean Hamish,' hissed back Alison. She struggled with the lid, but Hamish was straining against her. His strength was too much for her alone. 'I have to see for myself. Step aside. I'M HIS MOTHER!' she bellowed.

'No, not this love. Please. Go and sit down whilst I try and make sense of it all,' he begged.

Alison was vigorously shaking her head. Fresh tears were gushing down her cheek. 'But I have to see.'

Hamish knew his wife too well. She did have to see, otherwise she'd never rest well for the remainder of her life. 'Please, I beg you, don't look,' he pleaded one last time.

The head-shaking continued and she grasped Hamish's hands and removed them from the coffin. She then lifted the lid and leaned it against the wall. She looked down and gasped, 'Oh, good god, that's a, that's a,' she stammered.

Hamish cuddled her and tried to draw her away from the coffin, but she regained herself and started to shake her head and withdrew herself. She looked up to Paul's face and cradled it in her hands. 'He's so at peace. A few cuts and scratches, but he looks like he's asleep. My poor wee baby.' She leant down and kissed him on the lips, cheeks and forehead and then leant over to his right ear, 'I love you son,' she whispered. She stroked his hair and began singing softly, a long-forgotten nursery rhyme, humming over the words that she had forgotten, though the tune was well remembered.

Hamish went around her, so that his face was atop his son's, so that he could whisper into his wife's ears. 'Please stay like this love, sing Paul to sleep, I have to do something.' He didn't wait for a reply. He walked quietly around his wife and returned to the foot of the coffin. He looked down at what had distressed him. He willed himself to turn it over, or to pick it up. He grasped it and was so disgusted at the cold feel of it, at the exposed, cleanly cut bone, at the nerve endings and blood vessels that had been so almost surgically-like severed, that were jangling with his movements, that he dropped the severed hand. He had been surprised by the weight of it, but then events in Belize and elsewhere had come rushing back. He remembered how stunned he had felt at the weight of various body parts. Dizziness had threatened to overwhelm him, but he focused on the nursery rhyme, on the sweet sound of his wife's voice.

He willed himself to pick up the hand again, but the memories, long-forgotten and from distant lands, flooded his brain. He was back in the helicopter, back to when a Tornado jet's canopy had failed to blow off when the pilot had pushed the jettison button, moments before he knew that his plane was about to crash. He and his navigator had been thrown skywards, straight through the glass, plastic and metal frame of the aircraft, severing limbs, breaking bones, crushing heads, mashing brains and impaling torsos within explosive milliseconds. Their ejector seats forced the severed Royal Air Force men high into the air, burning them as they flew heavenwards. Their trajectory forced parts of them out of their flight suits, scorching the material into their remaining skin, down into their bones. They arced, lost momentum and dropped to the ground, scattering limbs, heads and torsos into a newly ploughed field.

Hamish had been part of the rescue team. They had been quickly briefed and scrambled. They had been expecting to retrieve wounded men, before rebel troops could seize them for their own nefarious ends. Instead, the helicopter had hot-landed whilst the Royal Air Force Regiment troops rushed out into a defensive position and shielded

Hamish and his fellow medic. Instead of a quick retrieval and the expected care in the helicopter, Hamish and his mate had to search around the field for as many body parts as possible, so that grieving mothers and wives had something to bury. It hadn't been a pleasant task, made more intense by the brief firefight that took place minutes after landing. Hamish's fear of helicopters had started then, whenever he heard the rotor blades whirring skywards when the oil rig workers were being ferried, or whenever a chopper appeared on TV or the cinema. His mind would rush back to the macabre jigsaw puzzle he had had to play out on the deck of an under-fire helicopter. A wave of emotional chilliness would bombard his every nerve and freeze him deep to the bone. Though he had prided himself that all body parts were retrieved and that masked rebels had not appeared on a foreign television screen or on YouTube broadcasting parts of a killed serviceman that would never have a dignified burial in the UK.

But now, with each movement of his son's coffin, caused by the regular stroking of Paul's mother to his hair, the hand's severed nerves twitched and squirmed, as if trying to move.

Hamish shook himself back to the present, back to his paternal and husbandly duty. He reached out to Alison and placed his arms around her. 'Come and sit-down love, I don't want you to see anymore. Close your eyes and come back to the chair.'

Alison ignored him. She continued to hum the nursery rhyme to her child, her first born, her baby Paul. All the while she stroked his hair, as if pacifying him from an uncontrollable bout of teething.

'Please love, come away with me,' insisted Hamish as he tried to prise her fingers from the cold head of their son.

She violently shrugged him off, shaking free from his grasp. As she bent back over and cradled her son's face, the satin covering unfurled and revealed more of his body.

Hamish gave a gasp as more flesh was uncovered, only he knew that it wasn't his son's, for there was a scalp between his legs. The severed hand had been turned over with the movement of the sheet, revealing a gang-type tattoo. 'There, there, is, is, a…' began Hamish as he started to hyperventilate.

'I'm not seeing it, I can only see Paul,' hummed Alison as she screwed tight her eyes and reached up and felt blindly for Paul's hair. She restarted her rhythmic stroking, more to calm herself now. Her humming of the nursery rhyme grew louder, as if to block out the hyperventilating and distress of her husband.

'What, why, what, is going on?' he screamed out as he pulled back the velvet sheeting and revealed his son's body. He was dressed in a blue silk shroud, but packed around his intact body was a head, frozen in a grotesque grimace, its mouth was drooped open, its lips a deep purple-blue, sagging towards Paul's left knee. There were other limbs, bones and even what looked like freshly-washed organs. He could make out a human kidney and even a heart.

Alison screamed back, 'I don't want to hear. I don't want to know. Make them go away. Take them away from our Paul. Make it right Hamish.' She gave a wail, an unearthly sound from the pit of her lungs, almost an ancestral scream, long forgotten from some base instinct. 'Please, please, please,' she beseeched over again, the nursery rhyme was now run out. All she could say were these begging words.

Hamish steeled himself to pick the cut limbs and body parts up, but the severed head drew his gaze in. Its open eyes seemed to move with each jerk of the coffin, caused by the shaking of Alison further up as she rocked and grasped its sides to keep herself upright. Hamish was mesmerised by them, almost as if they were hypnotising him. He could hear the whirring of the rotor blades to an imaginary helicopter as he once more found himself about to embark on a grisly cadaverous jigsaw puzzle. His hyperventilating grew worse and choked his speech, he could no longer form words and soon his breathing became a struggle.

Neither of them was aware of the door being quietly opened. A burly figure rushed in, followed by the wheezing undertaker. Both carried padded gauze swabs in their open palms. These were wet and purple-stained and were swiftly placed over the open mouths of Hamish and Alison. Hamish struggled violently as he was torn between helping his wife, trying to grab the screwdriver to use as a weapon and with trying to breathe. He flailed helplessly as he tried in vain to release the tight grip upon him. He then reached towards the coffin, as if beseeching Paul to wake up and help him, to help his mother. In his confusion, as his breath was suffocated, he took a weak hold of his son's coffin. Soon their struggled breathing relaxed and was softened just as their weight lessened and their grips on their son's coffin slackened. As husband and wife fell in unison into the expectant arms of the undertaker and his accomplice, Brendan wheezed out, 'You just had to look, didn't you? I warned you both, but no, you just had to open it up. Your son has been nothing but trouble for my family. Well, meet my son.'

The overhead light burned down onto Hamish's eyes and forced him awake. He groggily came too and gave himself a moment to process what he'd seen and what had just happened. He tried to sit up and struggled against unknown restraints. He failed. Though he knew that his eyes had been taped open, he tried to blink, to force much-needed moisture to his dry eyes, but he failed in this too. He couldn't even move his head away from the harsh glare and heat of the lights. He knew he'd been drugged. As he thought this, a familiar wheezing and rasping sound grew louder. Then there was a brief respite from the heat and light as Brendan's face flashed in front of him. It had on his face a wicked grin. His nicotine-stained fingers curled tight into his palms and he gave Hamish a serious of punches to his cheeks. One, two, three in quick and anger-filled succession.

Bones and cartilage shattered, and Hamish was unable to defend himself or reciprocate.

Brendan leaned back over Hamish's body, he was now running a scalpel carelessly over his chest and up towards his neck, it drew blood as it delved deep into his skin, as easily as a pathologist making an initial incision against an unyielding corpse. 'You just had to look, didn't you? You almost spoiled a great little operation that my son and I have. I thought you'd spotted our hidden camera, but that pretty little wife of yours distracted you.' He bent over and leered into Hamish's face. 'It's hidden in the flowers. We don't want your sort opening coffins. Not with what we pack away in them. You're the first to go against our advice. We usually just watch the others weep onto the wood of the coffins whilst we have a good laugh. You're the first to have spotted our hidden camera.'

Hamish tried to scream for help, but no sound escaped him. All he could do was lie there, immobile and helpless.

'We get all sorts of stuff from grateful clients,' continued Brendan as he stabbed the scalpel deep into Hamish's upper arm.

A kaleidoscope of torment burst through Hamish's body as he tried to bellow in rage and pain. His vision blurred and slowly refocused. He started to bleed onto the ceramic table that he was laid out on. He couldn't look down to see, but he was naked. His head rested on a block and at his feet was a drain, where his blood trickled to be collected by the undertaker's clinical waste receptacles.

Brendan relished the sound the scalpel made as it sucked out from the muscle of his victim as he withdrew it. He couldn't resist a delving twist as it came out. 'Oh, I'll be taking my time with you, don't you worry sunshine.' He leant forward again, eyes level with Hamish's. 'Just like my son will with that pretty wife of yours.'

Hamish felt his pupils widen and saw the relishing grin spread across Brendan's face.

'He prefers them warm, immobile and pliable to whatever position he fancies. Normally he'd take his pleasure in someone younger, but he told me he'd make an exception

for your wife. You see, he's not been around for a while.

He was helping the police with their enquiries. He got into

his car and drove when he shouldn't.' The grin became a

ghastly smile, followed by a wink. 'He took great care of

your son, helped him to the other side, so to speak.'

Hamish tried to cry out but just couldn't move.

'But don't you worry about a thing. We'll take good care

of you and your wife.' Brendan placed the scalpel onto the

ceramic table and gathered his hands together. He then

started to rub them, their steely fingers breaking the silence

of the room as they chaffed, whirred and turned. 'We've

another closed coffin funeral to arrange. We'll make sure

you're all together, well some parts of you,' laughed

Brendan as he ceased his habitual hand movements, turned

to reach for something and tipped out the ash contents of

Captain's small wooden urn over Hamish's face. The

cremated remains of the family dog scattered wide and some worked its way into Hamish's open mouth and eyes. His vision was obscured and as the dust settled it caused the undertaker to wheeze further and he doubled over in a gasping fit.

He took a few moments to compose his breathing and continued, 'You see, the local criminals have a profitable drug supply coming in on the fishing trawlers. And sometimes they need to get rid of some problematic competition. They can't always rely on being able to smuggle corpses or bits of them onto the boats to throw overboard at sea. That's where I come in. Nobody questions a closed coffin when the kindly undertaker tells the family that their loved one is not fit for viewing. They don't even question why their granny or son needs a longer or wider coffin. They just accept that I tell them about feet dropping. That way there is more space to pack away troublesome drug dealers. Oh, you'd be surprised as to how many policemen and even judges are addicted. Even mortuary assistants have a deep craving for what my friends supply.' He reached behind him, dropped the empty dog's ashes urn and lifted a shiny saw. He held it aloft, as if to admire its gleaming silver surface and fine blades in the light.

Hamish struggled and failed to wake his body up, his breathing was becoming more laboured as his lungs struggled with his beloved dog's ashes. Through the torture all he could think about was saving Alison from the monster that took their son from them.

Brendan paused thoughtfully, replaced the saw, and picked up a cuddly duck. He held it over Hamish's eyes. 'What a stupid thing to put in a grown man's coffin,' he mocked as he furiously pulled it apart. With one final tear, he then delved inside it and pulled out the stuffing. He gathered some up into a golf-ball sized amount and stuffed

it into Hamish's mouth. He turned back and picked up the

saw again. 'Even anaesthetists at our children's hospital

come running to us for a quick fix. And we get so much in

return, like muscle relaxants and knock out chemicals.

That's what you've had,' warned Brendan as he flashed

the saw across Hamish's vision. 'You won't be able to

move a muscle, but I'm led to believe that you'll feel every

bit of the sawing and cutting.' He laughed manically as he

quickly delved the saw across Hamish's inert body and

started to cut and saw through his skin, muscle, nerves,

blood vessels and finally his arm bones. 'Once we had the

mortuary assistant in our pockets, things got easier for us,'

Brendan casually explained as he sawed with minimal

effort. 'My son used to use a chainsaw.' He stopped his

sawing as if reminiscing, 'Can you imagine! O, what a

mess he made. Blood and bone everywhere.' He continued

sawing casually, as if carving a Sunday roast. 'But now we can have an arm clean off, within seconds!' he exclaimed as he lifted Hamish's bloody arm and held it aloft in triumph. 'And don't you worry about a thing, my son will soon get off on a technicality, just you see. The police officer writing the paperwork will have thrown something into the legal system so that he can have his nightly fix to get him through the horrors he sees in his dreams. And the lawyers will soon wangle my son free on that technicality and then the Judge will throw out the case. It'll be the one with the liking for underage prostitutes, or perhaps the one about to have an allegation of sexual harassment made against her by one of her colleagues. You see, all roads lead to the drug overlord. He's got so many in his pocket and enthralled by what he can provide. Even me. And I'm top of the food chain. Though I'm not long for this world, I've cancer and chronic emphysema. But the drug overlord, he makes sure that I'm pain-free as I continue my important work with my son. No-one will know you were here. Our CCTV will be unaccountably blank, and your car will already be in a container, ready to ship overseas tonight. Shame you didn't bring your daughter along, my son really does like them younger.'

Hamish slipped in and out of consciousness as fresh waves of pain overwhelmed him. Through his agony all he could hear, even above the sawing and Brendan's wheezing, was his daughter shouting, 'BUT YOU PROMISED!'

Dedicated to my dear son, Angus, forever 22 years old. And to every parent who has experienced the overwhelming and catastrophic loss of a child and has bravely put one foot in front of the other and waded through life without their cherished child and his or her unfulfilled promise and dreams.

Author's Note

Grief took me to some dark places when I lost my dear son, Angus. I didn't realise how ill I had become, though health-care professionals were telling me, as was my dear wife, Karla. My own PTSD, which I'd tried to manage for years, escalated out of control. The compassion of my daughter Abigail, my wife Karla, friends, a fantastic GP and an amazing NHS Psychologist helped to heal my fractured mind. Thank you all. During this time, this strange story unfolded in my brain. I hope you will forgive it dear readers. My next novel will be a sweet romance, no really it will be, honest, though a slasher story is creeping into my dark thoughts…

Follow its progress on social media whose links can be found at www.cgbuswell.com

If you liked this novel, then please leave a review at Amazon, Good Reads or on your social media. It will help me out a lot. Thanks! Chris.

Acknowledgments

My grateful thanks to my dear wife for being by my side during the most cataclysmic of times in our lives and for our beloved daughter, Abigail, who has given us a reason to go on with life. Thank you Karla for the wonderful cover artwork.

Ray and Katherine are the most cherished of friends and fantastic proof-readers. Thank you for knocking on the door when all we wanted to do was curl in a corner.

The kindness of strangers and charities has picked my daughter, wife and I from the floor, comforted, nurtured and guided us as we try to live our lives without our much-loved son and brother. These included SOBS and The Compassionate Friends. Thank you for the support group and for the bursary for the retreat.

Emily and Ian work tirelessly at SSAFA and tried to seek help from military charities and Associations to continue to soundproof my home when our savings ran out. Thank you for trying anyway.

Help for Heroes provided me with a most effective set of noise-cancelling headphones that shut out demented banging and are heavenly for a writer. Thank you so much.

Richard and Dawn of Holidays for Heroes Jersey restored our faith in humanity and are the sweetest, kindest people God has sent. Jersey is such a healing and peaceful Island, thank you for sharing it with Karla and I and for bringing us back within the military veteran's family.

Fiona, Lorraine and Kate of Bravehound have given me a reason to wake up in the morning and a buddy to help in the constant, tiring battle with PTSD. Lyn is gorgeous, great fun and is my new best friend! Words seem so inadequate when I try and convey how much you have changed my life. Thank you so very much.

Maria kindly gave Karla and I the privilege of staying in Daz's Den and experiencing the beauty of Mablethorpe. Bless you Daz's parents for helping another bereaved couple and for aiding countless wounded in mind and body, veterans and their families.

PTSD Resolution stepped in and extended their excellent counselling service when we had another family crisis. Thank you.

Anthony of John Paul Retreats is humble, caring and generously donates a flat on the Isle of Bute so that bereaved parents and siblings can find peace for their thoughts. I feel privileged to call you a friend.

Peterhead Food Bank fed and nurtured Karla and I when our savings ran out and I lost a major advertiser from my website work. Thank you for stopping us from starving whilst I found another source of income.

To everyone who donates to the charities I mentioned above or who fundraises, a big Thank You, without your kind donations and efforts I don't think that I would be here today. A percentage of my profits from this novel and others will be split between the above charities as I try and repay the kindness.

Thank you, Richard of Rogue Media, for formatting the book cover and for the lettering. As always, your work looks stunning.

And of course, a big thank you to you, dear reader, for reading my novels which I greatly enjoy writing. It's a form of mindfulness for me and very cathartic, I hope you don't mind.

Chris

Printed in Great Britain
by Amazon

41387355R00248